SAN RAFAEL PUBLIC LIBRARY
SAN RAFAEL, CALIFORNIA

Girl and horse plunged into the waves together and then they swam side by side.

The water wasn't deep, but Darby tipped forward with her arms outstretched. It made more sense to let Hoku draw her along.

Darby flew through sun shafts and shadows, shallows and depths. The ocean shifted from aqua to sapphire, from blue green to lime. Kelp and sea ferns waved at their passing.

With her face under water, she fought back a delighted laugh. Hoku was having the time of her life, swinging her legs so gracefully through the sea, she might have been born a water horse.

D1041419

Check out the

Phantom Stallion

series, also by Terri Farley!

SAN RAFAEL PUBLIC LIBRARY
SAN RAFAEL, CALIFORNIA

Welcome to

Phantom Stallion
WILD HORSE ISLAND

Phantom Stallion

WILD HORSE ISLAND 6

SEA SHADOW

TERRI FARLEY

HarperTrophy®
An Imprint of HarperCollinsPublishers

This book is dedicated to all who made readers of non-readers,
who will make more readers of more non-readers.

Disclaimer

Wild Horse Island is imaginary. Its history, culture, legends, people, and ecology echo Hawaii's, but my stories and reality are like leaves on the rain-forest floor. They may overlap, but their edges never really match.

Harper Trophy® is a registered trademark of HarperCollins Publishers.

Sea Shadow

Copyright © 2008 by Terri Sprenger-Farley

All rights reserved. Printed in the United States of America. No part of this book may be used or reproduced in any manner whatsoever without written permission except in the case of brief quotations embodied in critical articles and reviews. For information address HarperCollins Children's Books, a division of HarperCollins Publishers, 1350 Avenue of the Americas, New York, NY 10019.

www.harpercollinschildrens.com

Library of Congress catalog card number: 2007934247

ISBN 978-0-06-088619-6

Typography by Jennifer Heuer

❖

First Edition

6
SEA SHADOW

©Gary Chalk

TWO SISTERS VOLCANOES

MESSAGE
BOTTLE LANDING

'IOLANI
RANCH

RAIN
FOREST

SUN
HOUSE

OLD PLANTATION

TUTU'S
COTTAGE

CRIMSON
VALE

NIGHT DIGGER
POINT BEACH

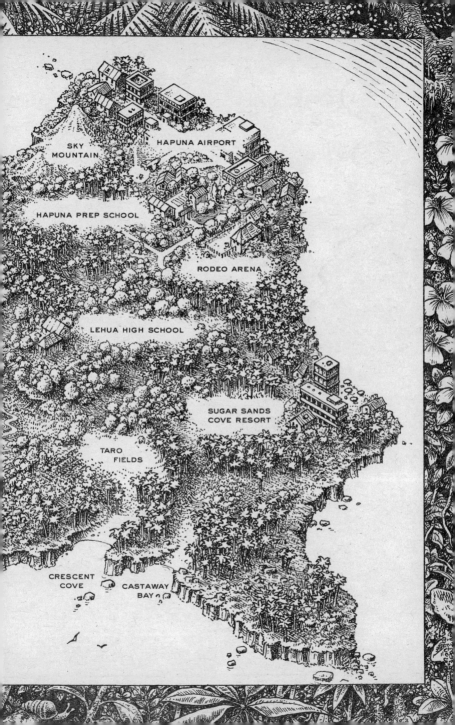

Chapter One

How did horses put up with riding in dizzying Tilt-A-Whirl horse trailers?

Darby Carter clung to the partition between herself and Hoku as the truck and trailer made a sickening swoop around a pond-sized puddle.

At first, it had seemed like a good idea to ride in the trailer with Hoku, so she could see firsthand how it felt. And from inside the truck, she couldn't read her filly's eyes or ears. So Darby had chosen this short drive from 'Iolani Ranch to Sugar Sands Cove Resort to give it a try.

Gazing through the open-sided trailer into the tropical forest, Darby decided a better question than how horses put up with such treatment was *why*?

They were bigger and stronger than the humans who asked them to go inside these wheeled torture chambers.

Hoku's neck wrinkled like sorrel satin as she turned to regard Darby. Blinking and chewing her hay, the filly looked puzzled by her human's staggering.

"I only have two legs to balance on," Darby explained to her mustang. "You can brace with all four."

Hoku swallowed. She kept her eyes on Darby's and her ears pricked forward for more conversation.

"Besides, horses must have a different sort of inner ear than humans. Otherwise, a rowdy girl like you would never get in a horse trailer for a second trip."

Hoku broke off their stare by nudging Darby's nose with her own.

Darby stumbled back, hit the far side of the trailer, and slid down to the floor. She rubbed her nose and considered the trailer from this new angle. It was a good thing she'd scrubbed every inch of it clean before deciding to ride back here.

The truck and trailer made another swoop and this time the maneuver not only left her stomach someplace back down the road, it sprayed her with muddy water. Darby wiped her cheeks and tried to visualize Sugar Sands Cove.

The trip would be worth it. After a week of rain that had turned 'Iolani Ranch into a swamp, the warm white beach would be heavenly.

She was still amazed that her grandfather, Jonah, had allowed her to get up early and do this before school. Once they arrived, there wouldn't be time to do much except unload Hoku and head for the waves.

Darby sighed. She never would have been able to go swimming with a horse before school when she lived in Pacific Pinnacles, California. Only on Wild Horse Island did things like this happen!

She was imagining the sandy warmth against her bare feet and Hoku's hooves, when dirt scratched the tires, pebbles pinged under the trailer, and the truck came to a halt that slammed her teeth together.

Enough.

"Cade!" Darby shrieked.

She'd been so eager to continue Hoku's sea schooling, she'd agreed to let the teenage cowboy drive.

"What are you doing?" she demanded when he didn't answer.

Jonah thought it was no big deal for Cade, who hadn't tested for his driver's license yet, to make short trips like this. Her grandfather often needed more help around the ranch than he had, so Cade did things like this all the time. Driving for agricultural purposes was even legal if he kept to the unpaved private roads belonging to 'Iolani Ranch.

Legal was one thing. Safe was another.

The truck door squeaked open. Why was Cade getting out of the truck?

Darby had opened her mouth to ask, when Cade's shadow blocked the sunlight streaming into the trailer.

"Stay down and stay quiet."

Hoku must have been as surprised as Darby, because the filly didn't flatten her ears or kick the tailgate.

Darby rarely obeyed orders without asking why, but this time she made an exception. Cade's grim whisper kept her seated and silent.

As Cade's boots moved away, Darby pictured the lanky guy with his blond paniolo braid tucked under his hat. She heard him striding around mud puddles, moving determinedly toward—what? An injured animal he didn't want her to see? A place where the road had washed out?

Darby calculated that they'd driven about halfway to Aunt Babe's resort. That meant they were passing near the taro fields.

Hoku's uneasy nicker muffled the sound of a second pair of feet.

"Good way to get run over, blocking the road like that," Cade said.

Who was he talking to?

Getting to her feet to peek out of the trailer was almost irresistible, but Darby managed to stay down.

"What's in the trailer?"

The oily voice made Darby glad she hadn't moved. Cade's stepfather Manny was out there. He owned the taro fields, so it made sense that he'd be in the area.

Logic didn't stop Darby's goose bumps.

Kimo had said Manny reminded him of a pit bull and Megan had said Manny's head looked like a coconut—round with dark, stringy hair.

Darby's mind didn't pull up a clear picture of Manny, just the information that he hurt horses and children, and the feeling that he was the scariest man she'd ever met.

Why had he decided to block the road? And why should he care what was in the trailer?

"Horse I'm taking over to the tourist trap," Cade said, and Darby could tell he thought that if he could get Manny to poke fun at Babe's fancy resort, he'd stay away from the trailer.

It didn't work.

"Which horse?" Manny's voice moved closer. His shadow blocked the light.

Hoku drew back in surprise, but just for a second. Nostrils flaring, she lunged, colliding with the metal wall of the trailer.

"That filly from Nevada."

This time Cade's casual tone sounded strained. Was he afraid Manny had seen her? Had he?

So what? Darby asked herself. Manny was a small, mean man who stole ancient Hawaiian artifacts and sold them on the black market. Not a kidnapper.

"The one with the white . . ."

Darby didn't catch the rest of what Manny said, but her gaze lifted to the white star on Hoku's chest, the marking she'd named her for, and she wished Manny hadn't known that detail about her horse.

"How'd Mom do in the earthquakes?" Cade asked.

He might be trying to distract his stepfather, but Darby heard the real concern in Cade's voice. Not that Dee deserved it.

Be fair, Darby told herself, but she couldn't.

She'd never met the woman who'd allowed Manny to beat Cade until his jaw was broken, but that was all Darby needed to know to dislike Cade's mom.

"Dee's fine," Manny spat, "but the house is a wreck. Roof came down on the lanai. Stuff broke. You'd think she was homeless the way she carries on."

"All you need to do is call the state. They'll come out and tag—"

"Yeah, I want the state digging into my business," Manny sneered. There was a moment of quiet interrupted by the agitated call of a bird, before Manny went on. "You know, your mom coulda been out of here, livin' in luxury on the mainland. It's your fault she's not. All you had to do was turn over that colt."

That colt?

Stormbird! Darby thought, and all at once she

remembered the midnight phone call she'd eavesdropped on from her bedroom. Jonah had called Cade in from the bunkhouse, telling him it was his mother. It probably had been, at first, but Darby remembered how Cade's tone had turned surly. She'd been sure, then, he'd been talking to Manny.

"I'm never putting any horse in your hands ever again."

"Like you have a choice."

If a venomous snake had a hissing voice, this would be it.

"You don't scare me," Cade insisted.

"Don't have to. I have title to that Appy of yours."

Darby knew that a title was a legal paper saying you owned something, like a boat or a car or a horse. She and her mother had gotten Hoku through the Bureau of Land Management's wild horse adoption program, and even though they'd been permitted to take the filly out of state, they wouldn't have legal title to her until after next Christmas.

Manny owned Joker. That was awful, but what did it have to do with Stormbird?

Darby could almost hear the thudding of Cade's heart as he thought about his horse. He loved Joker. She'd heard him call the Appaloosa "brother."

"Well, he's back with Babe now," Cade said.

He . . . they had to be talking about Stormbird again.

"Babe hasn't given you and your little girlfriends

the reward yet." Manny's wheedling tone made Darby grit her teeth. "That reward will buy you the title to Joker. He'll be yours, free and clear."

"I'll think about it," Cade said.

"Don't think small."

"What's that supposed to mean?"

"It'll take the whole reward to get your horse."

"But, it's a three-way split." Cade sounded confused.

"Stuff happens," Manny said.

Cade made a disgusted sound. "I'm *hanai*'d to Jonah. You agreed to that. And one of the girls is his granddaughter—"

"Saw her. Don't trust her."

He doesn't trust me? Darby pressed her hands over her mouth to smother her squeak of outrage.

"She'd be heartbroken to hear she don't have your admiration," Cade snapped, but that didn't stop Manny.

"Now, Mekana? Give her problems and she'd kick your butt. But that Darby girl's like a monkey, yeah? More going on in her head than she lets on— What was that?"

Darby didn't think she'd uttered a peep, but why else would Manny sound so suspicious?

"Never heard a filly squeal before?" Cade was making fun of his stepfather, but Manny's feet still moved closer.

As he approached, Hoku uttered a high-pitched

whinny. The whites of her eyes showed as she struck out a hoof in warning.

Good girl. Darby sent her thoughts flowing toward the mustang. *Smart girl.*

"Yeah, well"—Manny seemed to lose interest—"you know where to find me . . ."

"So I stay away," Cade told him.

". . . and I know where to find that Appy."

Darby thought she heard Manny leave on something like an all-terrain vehicle, but she wasn't going to make a move until Cade told her it was just the three of them again.

She'd been so still for so long, sitting with her arms wrapped around her knees, her joints felt stiff. But it gave Darby time to wonder what she'd do if she were Cade.

It was easy to forget he had been an abused child. Jonah had told her about seeing ten-year-old Cade running away from home. He'd been walking along the road, his broken jaw swollen to the size of a grapefruit, leading Joker with a belt around his neck. Not everyone who'd had that kind of treatment would turn out honest and hardworking like Cade.

But this was a tough decision. Making a decision between honesty and your horse was kind of a crossroad, and putting herself in Cade's position wasn't hard. She'd gladly give up her part of the reward, and try to persuade Megan and Cade to do the same, if it meant keeping Hoku out of the hands of a creep like Manny.

She looked up at her filly with a sigh.

Hoku's head nodded and her eyes were closed. The mustang was dozing, so the danger must be gone.

"You ready to ride up front?" Cade's voice was so close, it made Darby jump and Hoku snort.

Darby only hesitated for a few seconds. She wanted to have a good time with Hoku once they arrived at the beach, and that meant not feeling sick from the trailer's swinging and swaying.

"Yes," she said.

Besides, Cade might want to talk over his predicament.

A minute later, she was in the truck cab, seat belt fastened, sitting next to Cade as he drove.

Say something, Darby urged herself.

Cade leaned forward, chest touching the steering wheel as if he couldn't see the road. Or maybe he was trying to block her out.

Darby shrugged her shoulders up as high as they'd go.

"There's nothing to worry about," Cade chided her as if she were a little kid. "Really." He darted a glance at her. "No big deal."

What did he think she was, a baby? She recognized threats when she heard them. And from Manny, "I know where to find that Appy" was a threat.

"Yeah, right," Darby said. "He wants to take your horse!"

Eyes back on the road, Cade gave the same sort of humorless laugh she'd heard from Jonah.

"Let him try," Cade said.

Darby leaned against the seat back and crossed her arms. Wasn't that just like a guy? A cornered guy, she thought, but she didn't say it.

"Call the police," Darby suggested. "That's the obvious thing to do."

When he didn't say anything, she wondered if a small island like this even had a police force. It must. But maybe that's what had Cade worried.

"Or are you afraid—" she began.

"He doesn't scare me," Cade snapped.

"I meant," Darby raised her voice, thinking Cade had said those words way too often for them to be true, "are you worried that if the police get involved, he'll show them the title to Joker and they'll have to let Manny take him?"

Cade shook his head and slowed down as a car passed them, then returned to a normal speed.

But still he didn't answer.

Darby cleared her throat. Then, she looked out her window. Maybe if he didn't have to meet her eyes, he'd speak up.

"Manny's never had title to anything in his life," Cade said finally. "The house is Mom's. They rent most of the land. Except for groceries and gasoline, he gets everything through barter or blackmail. Unless he steals it."

"So . . . " Darby drew out the word. This was the hard part. "Are you going to try to get him the money?"

"Heck, no! Are you crazy? And he'd better keep away from you and Megan. I'll tell Kimo and Kit what he's up to, so they can watch him, too."

Darby squirmed against her seat belt. In a way it felt good to be watched over. But it also felt childish.

"I'll wait to tell Jonah until he gets back," Cade said.

Jonah was leaving the ranch for a few days, and so was Megan. In fact, they were both leaving the island.

Megan had earned a place on a class science trip to Oahu and Jonah was going at the same time, to look over a Quarter Horse stallion called Oreo Leo.

Her grandfather said he needed to diversify his horses' bloodlines, even though he was satisfied with foals sired by Kanaka Luna.

He didn't want a second stallion on the place, but chances to buy a horse like Oreo Leo didn't happen in Hawaii as often as they did on the mainland.

When Megan had grumbled to her mother that Jonah was taking the same flights so that he could spy on her, Aunty Cathy had said—pretty sarcastically for her—"Of course, Megan. Taking out a bank loan to buy a horse and ship it back to Moku Lio

Hihiu is a small price to pay for knowing what you're up to."

"Is that okay?" Cade asked now, as they made the last turn before Sugar Sands Cove Resort. "I don't think Jonah would leave for Oahu if he thought Manny was acting up, but Megan will be gone, and I don't think Manny will really—"

"Of course, it's okay," Darby said. "It's not like I need bodyguards. Right?"

"Right," Cade said.

Darby knew she'd just imagined that his voice held a trace of doubt.

Chapter Two

"This is the only part of the drive where I'm not quite legal."

Cade braked at the stop sign. As he looked left and right repeatedly, Darby couldn't help doing the same thing. To the left, the highway continued toward the town of Hapuna. To the right, the high-way was flanked with fields of black lava stone.

Darby rolled down her window, taking a closer look, and shivered a little. A few days ago she'd learned what newborn lava looked like up close, and it was scarier than those sharp black rocks.

Directly across the highway stood Sugar Sands Cove Resort. Cade looked ready to make his move, but he did nothing. Darby didn't point out that the time was right. There wasn't another vehicle in sight in either direction.

"Take your time," she told him. As long as Cade was pulling a horse trailer with precious cargo, he could be as slow and careful as he liked.

Darby looked back over her shoulder, turning as far as she could without getting strangled by her seat belt. She could only see a swatch of sorrel inside the trailer, but as Hoku shifted restlessly, breathing salt air and listening to the waves' splashing and crashing, Darby felt the filly's excitement.

Hurry! The demand charged through Darby as Hoku pawed her trailer floor.

Cade accelerated across the intersection, then stopped again on the other side. And waited.

The gates to the resort swung wide with a stately slowness, giving guests a long look at sparkling buildings so white they might have been molded out of sugar.

Darby had been to the resort three times before, but she was still awed by the way it rose from raked sands to stand silhouetted against the bright blue waters beyond.

Those waters were perfect for her to share with her horse, and that's why it was lucky that she, Cade, and Hoku weren't guests.

They were family. At least Darby was, since Babe Borden, who owned the resort with her polo-player husband Phillipe, was Darby's great-aunt.

Tutu, Darby's great-grandmother, had split her huge land grant on Wild Horse Island between her two very different offspring.

When the gate finally stood open, Cade drove through. He didn't wait long before muttering, "Not my style."

"You sound just like Jonah," Darby told him, and though she'd meant he sounded grumpy, Cade's quick smile said nothing would make him happier than to be like her grandfather.

But Cade's smile faded as a woman in high heels with a hibiscus tucked into her hair stepped right out in front of him, so mesmerized by the white beach, she didn't notice Cade had to steer the truck around her.

"It is a different kind of beautiful than 'Iolani," Darby conceded, but she couldn't blame the woman for being hypnotized by the beauty of the sand and sea. Darby felt the same way.

And there was more.

Hoku's whinny greeted the cremello horses running along their paddock fence. With coats in every shade from stark white to pale buttermilk, they looked like fantasy horses, ready to lift off the ground and gallop among the clouds.

"They're amazing," Darby said. She sneaked a quick look at Cade, but so far he hadn't reacted to the horses with indifference as Jonah had.

No, they weren't Quarter Horses—the breed

Jonah believed were the royalty of the equine world—but Darby still couldn't believe Jonah hadn't accepted Babe's offer to give the cremellos to him.

Who would turn down seven gentle, saddle-trained horses?

No one with a brain and five-thousand acres of pasture land, Darby thought with frustration. Unless you were her stubborn grandfather.

So what if Babe had "ulterior motives," as Jonah had said. All his sister wanted was for the ranch to take the horses as a dude string, so her guests could come to 'Iolani Ranch to ride.

Darby had heard that Babe's husband Phillipe had ordered a state-of-the-art gym built in place of the paddock.

"There are Flight and Stormbird!" Darby pointed out the cream-colored mare and her foal. Both had turquoise eyes.

Cade nodded. Allowing himself a smile at the colt's too-long legs and too-big ears, he said, "He's gonna be one huge horse."

Cade had just pulled the truck in beside a white Escalade when Babe Borden appeared.

With her window lowered, Darby heard her great-aunt talking to a couple dressed in tennis whites. And suddenly, looking at their crisp and spotless clothes, Darby was uncomfortably aware of the clothes she'd thrown on in the predawn darkness.

If she stood against the trailer, maybe no one

would notice that her jeans had a rip across the back of one thigh from crawling under a barbed-wire fence after Bart, the young and crazy Australian shepherd. The jeans weren't usually too short because she wore them with her caramel-colored cowgirl boots. This morning, though, she'd put on slippers—what she'd call flip-flops at home—because she was getting straight into the water and didn't want to struggle with her boots.

Her bright orange T-shirt was emblazoned with a California grizzly bear, the mascot of her old school. The problem with the shirt was that there'd been a misprint on the bear's eyes and he looked kind of like he was leering, instead of growling fiercely.

Even her mom had laughed when she'd seen it, and said, "I'm not sure I like the look in that bear's eyes."

But she was far away from home now, and no one would care. Besides, her great-aunt was talking about her.

"This is my great-niece and -nephew," Babe was telling the couple. "And I do mean great!"

Darby was surprised that Babe had called Cade her great-nephew, when he was not quite officially Jonah's adopted son. Cade's flush looked so pleased, as well as self-conscious, Darby gave Babe a mental round of applause.

Cade slipped out of the truck. Darby snagged a little daypack from the truck's floor and followed, closing the door quietly so that she didn't spook her horse.

She needn't have worried, though, because Hoku's attention was on Babe.

"You must see this lovely mustang from Nevada," Babe told the couple.

Despite her gold rings glinting with diamonds, Babe jiggled open the latch on the horse trailer before Cade could, then kept up her commentary on the filly. "Although she's still half wild, I must admit this filly is a testament to what the paniolo horse charmers in our family can do."

Babe made a remarkable picture, with her gauzy skirt and blouse billowing around her as she backed Hoku from the trailer and presented the mustang to her guests.

"Her name is Hoku. It's Hawaiian for 'star.'"

Flaxen mane fluttering, Hoku held her head high and showed off the handprint-sized marking on her chest.

With a laugh as jolly as Tutu's, Babe added, "You're a star in every way, aren't you, sweetheart?"

Hoku broke her pose to study Babe, then cautiously nuzzled her hand.

This time Jonah's wrong, Darby thought. He called his sister a shallow social climber, but Darby saw a woman who could have been a horse charmer like her brother, if she'd wanted to be one.

All at once, Darby realized time was ticking away.

She couldn't be late to school, and every minute she spent standing here was a minute she'd miss in the water with Hoku.

Babe darted a quick, assessing look at Darby's outfit. Maybe Babe would shoo them on their way. That would be the easy way out, but Babe didn't make a face or a remark. She was unruffled by Darby's grubby clothes.

Things had been pretty rugged on 'Iolani Ranch when Babe and Jonah were growing up. She couldn't condemn her great-aunt for wanting a life that was different from the one she'd had there.

According to Babe, as soon as she'd earned her driver's license, her eccentric father had sent her driving around the island to gather up road-killed animals. They'd served as food for the foxes he'd raised as a short-term moneymaking scheme.

Even Darby, who didn't consider herself a dainty girly-girl, couldn't imagine doing that.

And what had Babe said? Something like, *Nothing improves a girl's social status like being seen picking up road-kill.*

Feeling sympathetic, Darby walked closer to her great-aunt. She kind of wanted to kiss Babe on each cheek. But Darby just wasn't that Hawaiian yet.

As the guests walked away swinging their tennis rackets, Hoku spooked. The mustang hadn't forgotten that humans could carry weapons.

"Hoku wants her mom," Babe joked as she

handed the filly's halter rope over to Darby.

At last, Darby thought, as she talked to her horse. "It's okay, girl. You're fine."

Babe matched her manicured fingers together as she studied the filly.

"No, not an asset for the reward ceremony," Babe mused to herself. "There will be masses of men here."

"There will?" Darby said. Beatings by Shan Stonerow, her first "trainer," had taught Hoku to hate men, and though the mustang had begun realizing that not all men would hurt her, she still didn't trust them.

"Ample," Babe said. Then she pulled her gaze away from Hoku to give Darby a smile. "Enough to upset her."

Darby nodded. The "reward ceremony" involved her, Cade, and Megan.

Babe Borden had always planned to use the recovery of her orphan foal as publicity for the resort, just as she had the posting of the reward. That Stormbird had been rescued by three local teenagers made the story even better, and Babe hoped travelers nationwide would hear all about it.

"Mark Larson, the TV reporter who did such a great job covering Stormbird's disappearance, is something of a horse nut," Babe confided. "He's coming this weekend to do a piece about horseback riding on the beach, and scouting camera locations for the ceremony while he's here."

Darby, Megan, and Cade had all agreed to go

along with Babe's ceremony, even though Cade's shyness almost made him refuse. Now, hearing about the TV reporter, he must feel even more uneasy.

Until she'd overheard Manny threatening Cade, Darby had known exactly what she wanted to do with her reward money. She'd planned to fly her mother over from Tahiti, where Ellen Carter was shooting a movie, for a visit. Darby secretly hoped that her mother would fall in love with her island home all over again.

Now Darby wasn't so sure. If Cade needed the money to keep his horse . . .

". . . don't you think?" Babe was saying.

Darby tried to pull her thoughts together. They'd been walking toward the beach, with Babe on one side of Hoku and Darby on the other. Cade followed along behind, out of Hoku's sight, but they'd all just stopped by the cremellos' paddock.

Darby was fidgeting, eager to get to the waves, when she noticed Babe staring into her eyes.

"Sorry, what?" Darby asked sheepishly.

"The cremellos. They'll be photogenic enough for the camera crews?"

"Sure they will," Darby said. "Flight looks amazing."

Babe gazed at the mare standing in the paddock between them and Stormbird.

"She's looked better," Babe said, then pulled her sunglasses down to cover her eyes and kept walking with Darby and Hoku toward the beach.

Darby reminded herself that this was the same woman who'd looked at Flight's jutting ribs and hollow eyes a few weeks before and insisted, "I have to find her colt or she's not going to make it."

What was it with Jonah and Babe not wanting to show their feelings? The rest of the Kealohas—well, Darby's mom, Tutu, and herself, at least—didn't act that way.

Babe's plans for the media event included ribbon dancers and hula experts, music, food, and giving notice to Pele, the volcano goddess, that there were to be no earthquakes.

She didn't look like she was kidding, Darby thought.

"How will you do that?" Darby asked.

"Of course no one puts Pele on notice," Babe said, "but I've been keeping track." She gave a concerned sigh. "I've been watching weeks of little unfelt earthquakes recorded on instruments underwater by the Pacific tsunami website—"

"Tsunami?" Darby gasped. Sure, she'd read that earthquakes and volcanic eruptions came to the islands one after the other. But even though tsunamis sometimes followed, she'd read that they were rare.

"There's no sign of anything, but I can't be too careful," Babe told her. "Any warnings and I've got to get all my guests evacuated, whether they want to go or not. . . ."

Fidgeting with the daypack she'd slung on, Darby wondered why tsunamis couldn't just be part of island stories. Pele, the fire goddess, and her sister, the sea goddess, didn't really have fights. The volcano didn't really mean to throw lava into the ocean, so why must the sea strike back?

". . . if there is a tsunami, I do not want reporters to just happen to be here for our event—'film at eleven' of a wave dashing against my beach, or . . ." As Babe glanced at her hotel, the sun turned her short black hair silver. "It would be disastrous. I'm not the sort who believes any publicity is good publicity." She gave Darby a half smile. "There's more to this innkeeper stuff than you thought, isn't there?"

Darby nodded, but her mind was filled with towering blue waves.

Suddenly, Babe asked, "Have you two eaten? For breakfast we have an ahi tuna with eggs."

Darby was still thinking tsunami, not tuna, but Cade answered with a grateful nod.

"Thanks, ma'am, but we ate."

"Cade," Babe said thoughtfully. She stopped walking and stood with one hand on the hip of her white skirt. "You could persuade Jonah to take the cremellos right after the event."

"Well, I don't know . . ."

"I promised Phillipe," Babe protested.

Even though Cade had kept his distance from

Hoku, when he cleared his throat, the mustang flattened her ears.

"I'll try," Cade said.

Babe relinquished her position beside Hoku to swoop over and kiss Cade on each cheek.

"Mahalo nui loa!" she thanked him, then waved and returned to her hotel.

Cade stared after Babe, looking a bit bewildered, but Darby turned to her horse. Hoku tugged at her lead rope, eager to plunge into the waves. Darby felt her heart speeding up to match the wild filly's.

The beach was still empty. Now was the time to rush into the ocean and crest the waves beside her horse. Before they had any audience but Cade, she wanted to swim next to her filly, peer underwater, and see what Hoku saw.

Darby glanced at Cade. He was watching her now, and he looked amused. Her excitement must show.

"We're wasting time," Darby said, and she took long strides toward the water before Hoku could pull her right out of her slippers.

Chapter Three

Darby kicked off her slippers at the water's edge.

It wasn't easy to wriggle out of her jeans, shed her T-shirt, and disentangle herself from her daypack at the same time she kept a grip on Hoku's lead rope, but Darby managed.

"A snorkel and mask," Cade mused once he spotted them.

Darby tried to read his expression. Did he think it was a dumb thing to do? Or disrespectful of Hoku?

"I know they aren't what most riders wear," Darby started making an excuse.

"Not most folks around here, but then" — Cade rubbed a hand over his mouth, trying to hide his smile — "you're not from around here, are you?"

"I—"

"Or maybe they're for Hoku?"

He was just joking, and that she could take.

"Here's the thing," Darby said. "It's kind of like riding in the trailer. When we were here before, Hoku swam with her head underwater, blowing bubbles and looking around, and she seemed to be having so much fun . . ." Darby let her voice trail off.

If she couldn't see the undersea world through Hoku's eyes, she at least wanted to see what the filly saw and imagine what a wild horse from Nevada thought of this range with blue water and kelp in place of sky and sagebrush.

But would Cade understand? So far, he hadn't made any cracks about her being a horse charmer. But if he was going to, this seemed like the perfect time.

Before he could, Darby said, "It might sound silly to some people, I guess."

"You're doin' good with her," he said, "so 'some people' can go hang."

"Thanks," Darby said, but she hadn't reveled in the compliment for more than a second when a far-off rushing sound made her look around.

She couldn't see where it was coming from, but she had a good idea what it was. All over the ranch and school, the ground was saturated. Water ran off hillsides into low spots or off edges, making small waterfalls. Here, it was running into the sea.

Probably she shouldn't feel nervous about Babe's referring to tsunamis, but she couldn't help it.

Cade had folded his arms and shifted his weight onto one foot. White sand salted his brown leather boots. His patience encouraged her to blurt, "Is there going to be a tsunami?"

"We have tsunami alerts all the time." Cade gave a dismissing wave. "You've seen all those signs, yeah?" Cade pointed.

When Darby's gaze followed his gesture, she realized she'd walked by so many of the pictographic signs showing people climbing uphill to escape waves, she didn't really see them anymore.

"Cathy's always checking 'em on her computer, too," Cade went on, "and when they come in—and they almost never do—they're not even up to your knees. Usually."

The brown face beneath the hat brim reassured her. Cade was a paniolo, a Hawaiian cowboy. Like most cowboys, he said things straight out. He wouldn't shrug off danger, or expect her to.

Okay, Darby decided, *I can handle that.*

And she wouldn't give one more moment of thought to the hot bounding boulders and fire showers of Two Sisters' eruption, which officials had labeled "minor."

Darby's gaze rested lovingly on Hoku. *This is your fault,* she thought. *Some people begin to worry all the time when they have kids. I worry about you!*

Aloud, she told Cade, "Thanks. That helps."

Hoku broke from a standstill into a trot and Darby stumbled, trying to keep up. Just as she did, the filly pricked her ears back toward the hotel.

Tropical music was wafting from the resort.

Cade heard it, too.

"Go before you have company," he said, nodding at the ocean. "Don't want to explain to rich folks what you're doin'. They'll want to do it, too."

"Why, Cade, I think you'd make a great hotel beach boy," she teased. "Or, what do you call them? Yeah, a cabana boy! You could bring people fruit drinks with little umbrellas in them and rub on their sunscreen—"

"Just go," Cade said, and even though Darby couldn't see his brown eyes in the shade of his hala hat, his smile said he was glad she'd cheered up.

So was Hoku. The filly pranced, splashing into the waves, rejoicing that her sorrel coat was beaded with water.

How could plain old water be so beautiful? Darby wondered. On Hoku, the droplets looked like mysterious jewels that might be called bay amber or chestnut topaz, maybe even horse diamonds.

Girl and horse plunged into the waves together and then they swam side by side. It was only when Hoku ducked her head in the ocean that Darby struggled into her snorkeling gear.

One look sent Hoku lunging sideways, creating a

current that pulled Darby after her, under the water.

Darby resurfaced, sneezing, but she coughed out a few words so Hoku knew it was still her.

"Don't you like the look of my new face?" she asked her horse. Carefully, she lifted the edge of the mask. As water dribbled down her cheeks, Hoku gave an uncertain rumble.

Dummy, Darby scolded herself. She should have known the mask would spook the horse. It might magnify her eyes. That, added to the accordion-ribbed tube that fit into her mouth and stuck up above her hair, probably made her look like a huge bloodsucking insect.

Darby smooched at her horse and held out her free hand.

"It's okay, Hoku, girl. It's just me," Darby said.

Hoku moved a few steps closer. Head held so low that her mane floated on the water's surface, the filly peered through her damp forelock.

With a watery sigh, Darby managed to tighten her dripping black ponytail.

Hoku lifted her head and rolled her eyes. She thought there was something seriously wrong with her human, but at least it was still her.

Hoku gave a snort that said maybe things would be okay, and then she ran. Her strides were slowed by the water. Surging parallel to the beach, she towed Darby along with her.

The water wasn't deep, but Darby tipped forward

with her arms outstretched. It made more sense to let Hoku draw her along. She'd never keep up with her horse if she tried to jog on the sandy sea bottom.

As Hoku headed for darker water, lifting her hooves to swim, Darby tried what she'd been dreaming about. She lowered her face until it was wet. She drew breaths through the snorkel, and then she widened her eyes as the mask became a window to the world under the sea.

The filly swam in a lazy drifting way and so did Darby.

Totally relaxed, Darby forgot her trailer-queasy stomach just as Hoku forgot the humans with threatening tennis rackets. Their scare on Two Sisters' volcanic slopes receded.

With only a month of school left to go, surely her mother wouldn't . . .

As Darby's forehead parted a veil of seaweed, she pushed troubling thoughts away. Later was soon enough to worry about what her mother would or would not do.

Hoku swam faster.

Darby flew through sun shafts and shadows, shallows and depths. The ocean shifted from aqua to sapphire, from blue green to lime. Kelp and sea ferns waved at their passing.

Far off to her right, Darby saw a place that looked bleached and pale to her undersea eyes. Something moved, there, in a cove.

It was . . . was it? Yes! A sea turtle was swimming over to inspect them. She couldn't tell if the golden crinkles were made by wandering sunbeams, or if its skin was marked that way.

Darby did her best to hang motionless in the water.

With a flick of its flippers, the turtle banked into a better viewing angle. It scrutinized girl and horse with wise eyes before stroking away.

Wow, a *honu*, Darby thought, grinning until the mask tightened on her face. And *honus* were Megan's *'aumakua*. That had to be a good sign, didn't it?

Darby was so excited, she forgot to keep her snorkel above the water and inhaled a mouthful of it.

Choking and sputtering, she bobbed up for air. The saltwater burned her nose and throat. Dog-paddling, Darby realized she and Hoku had moved into waters over her head. Clearing the water from her mask and wiping it from her eyelashes, she could still see Cade on the beach.

He gave a discreet wag of his hand. It couldn't be time to go back yet, so he must be waiting for her to climb onto Hoku's back.

Not yet, she wanted to yell, but that would disturb Hoku, so Darby just returned Cade's wave before turning to the open sea.

The dip of an oncoming wave took her deeper than usual. The white crest lifted her higher, too. At least, that was how it felt. And it was tricky regaining her bearings.

The ocean didn't have a consistent horizon. For a second she felt dizzy, trying to fix on something out there, when nothing stood still. She refused to let her sickness from the trailer return, but it was almost as if it shifted away from her, as if a giant had taken a drink of water.

What was that? The wake of another turtle? Just Hoku pulling her along?

Darby closed her eyes and stifled her shiver.

The lead rope tightened around her fingers. Bubbles tickled her legs. When she opened her eyes, wrinkles arrowed away on the water's surface. Hoku was moving again.

This time, with her face under water, she fought back a delighted laugh. Hoku was having the time of her life, swinging her legs so gracefully through the sea, she might have been born a water horse.

Finally, Darby and Hoku staggered ashore.

The saltwater felt thick. It clung to her thighs, knees, calves, and heels, trying to keep her from leaving.

Even Hoku carried her head lower than usual. She huffed through her nostrils, weary from her swim.

On the beach ahead, Cade seemed to have plenty of energy. He was putting it all into pacing.

"You feel that little quake?" he asked when she got close enough to hear.

"Is that what it was?" Darby gasped, trying to catch her breath to ask more.

"Let's go." Cade gave her a towel, then began walking back toward the hotel and the truck.

"Okay," Darby said. They were due back at the ranch in time for her to ride to school with Megan, so she hurried to catch up.

She held tight to the sandy lead rope and tried to pull her jeans on, but her wet legs made it impossible. They hung up on her feet, then stuck to her ankles.

She gave up on the jeans, but managed to get into her T-shirt. She maneuvered her salt-sticky toes into her slippers, carried her jeans, and jogged after Cade.

They closed the distance quickly and, for once, Hoku didn't fight the nearness to Cade.

Before they caught up with him, Darby glanced at her horse. Ears flattened, the filly stayed in step, the lead rope hanging slack between them. What was Hoku thinking? Maybe the filly had decided that if Cade brought her to the sea, he was a necessary evil.

Either that, or she was closing in to give him a nip.

"I'll go start the truck and back it around," Cade said over his shoulder.

"Okay," Darby said while nodding, glad he was determined to return quickly. It would give her time to get dressed for school.

Oddly, now that Cade was farther away, Hoku

slowed her steps and hung back at the end of her lead rope. Darby made a clucking noise. The filly stepped out, but cautiously.

Because she was concentrating on Hoku, Darby almost missed the hotel guests standing on the path ahead.

"Oh, what a pretty horse!" A pigtailed child jumped up and down and asked, "Can I pet her?"

"Take it easy, Heidi. Don't scare the horsey."

The man with the little girl—he must be her dad by the routine way he scooped her up, then positioned her astride his shoulders—approached with a smile.

"I know horses," he said. "She'll be fine with me."

Which she? The child, or Hoku? Darby didn't know, but she felt the tension building in her filly. Hoku was trying to make sense of a man with an arm-waving human hat. Each breath the horse drew came in louder.

"I'm sorry." Darby searched her mind for the right thing to say.

How many times had she done the same thing, approaching unfamiliar horses and riders at parades, shopping center openings, even police horses on duty?

"She's in training, I'm sorry," Darby said again.

"And she kicks," Cade called from the truck.

The little girl frowned and stuck a finger in her mouth.

"She kicked me," Cade went on, but he stopped short of showing off the permanent bruise Hoku had given him.

Thank goodness, Darby thought. But the little girl's lower lip trembled. Darby cast about for an idea to keep the girl from crying as she clung to her father's forehead.

"If you go right over to that paddock," Darby said, pointing, "you'll find some beautiful cremello horses. They're totally acclimated to people, even the mare with the foal."

"You hear that, Heidi? Shall we go visit the baby horse?"

"Uh-huh."

"Let's go check them out," the man said, and as he turned, he gave Darby a thumbs-up.

Darby was feeling pretty self-satisfied, and she thought Cade approved, too.

"You're the one who should work here," he said. Darby was shaking her head modestly when he added, "But first you'd better clean up your mouth."

"What?" Darby yelped as she latched the horse trailer behind Hoku.

"Paddock. Cremello. Acclimated!" Cade gave a short laugh. "You don't suppose that little girl under-stood?"

Darby shrugged her shoulders up to her earlobes and thought of lots of embarrassed excuses, but her mind wouldn't let them escape her mouth.

Cade was already seat-belted in and ready to go when Darby swung open the passenger door. She put one foot up on the truck, but before she climbed in, she said, "That's how I talk."

For a minute, Darby was only aware of the truck idling and Cade staring at her.

"Good for you," he said, sounding like he meant it.

Darby sat back in her seat with a sigh, feeling happy and drowsy while Cade turned on the truck's radio and started scanning for earthquake news.

 Chapter Four

As Darby climbed out of the truck back at 'Iolani Ranch, she saw Megan, ready for school, coming down from her upstairs apartment.

"I'm hurrying!" Darby yelled, and though she didn't have time to blow-dry her hair as she'd wanted, she was back out in front of Sun House in just a few minutes to pile into the backseat with Megan.

As they drove away from the ranch, Aunty Cathy looked up in the rearview mirror and met Darby's eyes. "Are you shivering?"

"A little," Darby said.

"Mom, her teeth are chattering," Megan said.

"I'm s-sitting right here," Darby said.

"Are you sick?"

"No, my hair's wet and—well, I did ride in the back of the horse trailer and that made me a little queasy," Darby admitted, but she didn't bring up the weird sea current, because she and Cade hadn't heard anything on the radio about another earthquake and she didn't want Megan and Aunty Cathy to think she was getting paranoid. Even though she sort of was.

"Mom! What are you doing?" Megan yelped.

Aunty Cathy had pulled into the drive-through lane of an expensive coffee place by Lehua High School.

"I'm getting Darby some hot chocolate to warm her up and settle her stomach."

"Oh my gosh!" Megan flounced as much as her seat belt allowed. Her cherry Coke–colored hair flapped up like wings. "You would never do that for me!" She leaned forward to catch her mother's eye. "Would you?"

"I might," Aunty Cathy said.

Carrying paper cups of hot chocolate, which they managed not to spill getting out in front of the school, Darby and Megan just made it as the first bell rang.

"Hey!" Ann Potter, Darby's newest and best friend in Hawaii, was being dropped off at the same time. "We'll be late together." Ann made a clunky pirouette in her cowgirl boots, then caught Darby in a one-armed hug. "You're all wet!"

"Just my hair. I was riding Hoku at the beach," Darby began, and after they waved Megan off to her first class, Ann and Darby talked about horses all the way to English.

Darby dropped her cup in a wastebasket before Miss Day could reprimand her for bringing food into the classroom, but it turned out that the first words from her teacher were actually pretty great.

"Very nice work," Miss Day said as she placed a graded essay test facedown on Darby's desk.

It had been their first in-class writing assignment. They'd had fifteen minutes to brainstorm which three people from all of history they'd most like to meet. Then, Miss Day had set a timer and they'd written the best paper they could in thirty minutes.

Darby lifted a corner of the paper.

An A.

Wow! That matched hot chocolate for lifting her spirits. Darby wanted to dance with delight, but she only smiled.

She was still smiling when she got to her Creative Writing class.

Lots of kids called the teacher, Mrs. Martindale, a witch, and many thought it was unfair that she saved the fun stuff—writing short stories, poems, and plays—for Creative Writing 2, which you had to be a junior or senior to take.

But Darby had never taken a creative writing class before, so she was satisfied doing metaphor, simile, and personification worksheets.

She had to admit, though, as the teacher began

handing back their first two-page assignment, that she was looking forward to another A.

For this assignment, they'd written a description of one of several photographs. Darby had almost chosen one of a spooky-looking Victorian house, and then she'd considered a snapshot of an old woman dressed like a pixie. But she'd finally settled on a black-and-white photo of a lonely-looking Hawaiian child.

Unlike Miss Day, Mrs. Martindale returned Darby's paper faceup.

The grade, neatly printed in red, was impossible to misread. It was an F. If the assignment hadn't had her name on it, in her own handwriting, Darby wouldn't have believed it was hers. Slashed across the body of the paper in red ink, the teacher had written: PLAGIARISM!

Darby's trembling fingers had a hard time gripping the edge of the paper to turn it over. When she accomplished that, she glanced guiltily around. No one else had seen it.

When they broke up into small groups to discuss synonyms for the word *said*, Darby was still dazed, and quieter than usual.

Plagiarism. That meant copying something and presenting it as your own work. Any fourth grader knew that. All Darby's former teachers had insisted it was better to skip an assignment and earn a zero than to plagiarize.

At her school in Pacific Pinnacles, teachers had warned that they used some kind of computer software to detect those who plagiarized work.

Darby tried to catch Mrs. Martindale's attention, but the teacher was busy at her desk in the front of the room. Mrs. Martindale wore her champagne-colored hair swept up and heavily sprayed. Her glasses were the same metallic color as her hair. So were her lipstick and her fingernails.

I never called you a witch, Darby thought, staring at the teacher who refused to meet her eyes, *so why did you call me a cheater?*

Maybe Mrs. Martindale hadn't had time to use that computer program on this assignment.

Finally, when the bell rang, Mrs. Martindale looked up. She dismissed the class without glancing at Darby, and all her morning shakiness came back.

Darby was terrified to talk to the teacher, but she had to at least try.

After everyone had left the room, Darby stood, steadied herself, then walked to the front of the room.

"Mrs. Martin—" She had to clear her throat to be heard. "Mrs. Martindale, I didn't cheat. I didn't copy this." Darby still couldn't get her voice above a whisper.

Pointedly, the teacher pushed her glasses up her nose, then raised her eyebrows, but she didn't say anything.

Was Mrs. Martindale waiting for her to confess?

"I know you don't know if you can trust me because I'm new, but you can."

It sounded lame, but it was all she could come up with, and it was the truth. She had plenty of other faults, but she didn't cheat.

The teacher sighed, removed her glasses, and tapped them on the desktop.

"I was hoping for an apology. I like you, Darby. Take your F and learn from it."

Darby's mouth was so dry, she almost didn't get the next words out. "At my old school, they had a computer program that scanned for plagiarism."

Mrs. Martindale looked at her for so long, Darby imagined the teacher would say something sarcastic, like "This isn't your old school," or, "So you've been accused of plagiarism before, have you?"

Instead, Mrs. Martindale said, "The English department talked about getting that software, but this is a small school on a small island. Our budget just wouldn't stretch that far."

At the sound of shuffling feet, they both looked toward the classroom door. Students from the next class were waiting to come in, and Darby knew she was about to be late for Algebra.

Mrs. Martindale stood up. "Let's just move on and forget this happened, shall we?" She motioned for the waiting students to come inside.

Without nodding or agreeing, Darby edged past the other kids and plodded toward Algebra. She couldn't make herself hurry.

Forgetting it had ever happened would be the best she could hope for if she'd done something wrong, but she hadn't.

"Are you sure you're okay?" Ann asked Darby for the third time.

"I'm sure," Darby told her friend, but she wasn't okay. She should have gone back after school to talk to Mrs. Martindale again. She kept thinking about telling Cade this morning, "That's how I talk."

Why hadn't she been as firm and confident with Mrs. Martindale?

Now it was too late.

Lehua High was miles behind her and she hadn't told Ann about Mrs. Martindale's accusation because Ann would want to charge in and do something about it herself.

Ann's dad had just stopped his car at 'Iolani Ranch to let her out.

"I'm fine, really," Darby said. "Just hot."

"This morning you were cold," Ann said, nodding at the hooded sweatshirt she was still wearing.

Darby had borrowed it from Ann, and she should have given it back by now. But ever since she'd tucked her two graded assignments, folded tightly together, into the sweatshirt's front pocket, Ann had been with her.

Darby had kept her hands in the pocket, making

sure the papers didn't fall out.

"It's a crazy climate," Ed Potter, Ann's father, said.

Both girls made sounds of agreement as Darby climbed out of the car and hesitated next to it, trying to smile.

Darby wished she'd told Ann. It would have been a good rehearsal for telling her mom and Aunty Cathy. And Jonah.

"You got everything?" Mr. Potter asked, scanning the car's backseat.

"Yep," Darby said.

"Okay, then," Mr. Potter said. "We'll see you Sunday for the grand launch."

Ann rolled her eyes at her father's description of putting his new boat in the water.

"And feel free to bring Megan," Mr. Potter added.

"Thanks, but she and Jonah are leaving for Oahu right after she gets home from school"—Darby stepped closer to the car—"and I don't think they're getting back until Tuesday."

She skimmed her fingers back and forth on the window ledge, trying to think of something else to say to Ann.

"I told you what they named it, right?" Ann asked.

Darby shook her head, even though she had.

"*The Sage Sailor*," Ann said, pretending to stick her finger down her throat.

"What else would a family from the Sagebrush

State name their first boat?" Mr. Potter scoffed at his daughter.

"I'll stick with horses," Ann said, "but at least it's a good excuse for a party."

Finally, Darby stepped back so that the Potters could leave.

"See you Sunday!" Ann said, waving a hand out the car window.

"See you Sunday," Darby replied with a weak wave of her own, and then she trudged toward Sun House, hoping she didn't meet anyone on her way.

Chapter Five

Darby stopped on her way to Sun House, pausing to stare across the bluff to Upper Sugar Mill pasture. Two tiny figures that might be Kimo and Kit were working with cattle. Her pause gave Jonah a chance to call her into the office.

The ranch office sat right next to the house. It had a concrete floor, filing cabinets, two desks, a computer, and a fax machine. Nothing special, except that where most offices had a front wall, this one was open to the weather.

Inside, Jonah was bothering Aunty Cathy as she was trying to get back to work. The ranch manager had taken a short time off after she suffered a concussion in the strongest of the many earthquakes that had rumbled through the island in the last few weeks.

Some of the ranch dogs—Jack, Jill, and Sass—frolicked around Darby's ankles, following her into the office.

"I didn't call you," Jonah greeted them. "Out."

Slinking as if their spirits were broken, the dogs walked a few yards away, then flopped down in the shade. They kept their ears pricked toward the office, waiting for Jonah to change his mind.

"I have an extra hour because Megan's getting a ride home with a friend, but Jonah's making my job impossible," Aunty Cathy complained as Darby came out of the bright day into the dim coolness of the ranch office.

According to her doctor, Aunty Cathy had recovered from the concussion.

She looked like herself again. Her bruises and light-headedness had vanished and she'd brushed her blond-brown bob until it cupped her face to show off her healthy color.

But Jonah disregarded the doctor's diagnosis and wouldn't stop coddling Cathy Kato.

"Someone's got to help you ease back into your job," Jonah said.

"You're not helping," Aunty Cathy objected. "You're getting in the way."

It was easy to see that the two adults were driving each other crazy and Darby would bet Aunty Cathy saw only one good thing about Jonah's interference.

He was taking her place as chaperone on Megan's science trip to Oahu. Aunty Cathy would get some real rest while he was gone.

Darby gave her grandfather a puny smile, but he was flipping through a file folder and didn't notice.

Do it now, Darby told herself. This was the perfect time to just settle on the office couch and calmly tell Jonah and Aunty Cathy about Mrs. Martindale's mistake.

She'd probably get levelheaded advice from both of them, unlike the flare of mother-bear protectiveness she'd get if she called her mom.

Just then, Darby heard a nicker. It sounded like Hoku, but it was too close to be coming from the filly's corral, down past the old fox cages.

"Help me find our plane tickets," Jonah said.

"Somehow the printer was allowed to run out of ink while I was recovering," Aunty Cathy explained, as if she were mystified. "But Jonah's convinced that he printed out the confirmation e-mail."

"What time does your flight leave?" Darby asked.

"It's in here," Jonah insisted.

"Seven," Aunty Cathy answered.

The nicker came again.

"Is that Hoku?" Darby asked, edging toward the door.

Aunty Cathy nodded. "After I unloaded her, Jonah asked me to tie her at the hitching rack."

"Get her used to being in the middle of things,"

Jonah said, without looking up.

"And she's been there all day?" Darby asked. "How's she doing?"

"She hasn't stirred up a fuss," Jonah said, then shouted, "Ha! I told you!"

Cathy was mumbling about wonders never ceasing when Darby escaped the office to go see her horse.

Hoku's long, throaty neigh made Darby want to run to the mustang and fling her arms around her neck, but Jonah was coming out of the office behind her, so Darby resisted.

Approaching her horse, Darby slowed her steps. Something about the hitching rail looked different. It was a typical *H* shape with a long bar in the middle for tethering horses. She couldn't have said what had changed. Shrugging, she decided it was just that Hoku was tied near the right post.

"Isn't anyone paying attention to you?" Darby asked Hoku.

When the filly danced almost on tiptoe for her attention, Darby forgot about everything else.

"She's not a pet," Jonah reminded her.

Hoku wore the same halter and lead rope she'd had on that morning. The salt-stiff lead rope was tied to the crosspiece of the hitching rail. Usually, horses wore a neck rope and that was used to tie them.

Maybe that's what I noticed, Darby thought.

"Is that right?" she pointed as she asked Jonah.

"It's not wrong, since she's not wearing a bit and bridle," he said, frowning. "But she should get used to the other. Find a neck rope."

Inside the tack room, scents of leather and saddle soap surrounded Darby.

Outside, Hoku gave an angry squeal. The sound was a sure sign Jonah had ventured too close. So Darby hurried, reaching up to snag a neck rope that was hanging from a hook.

Silken rustling made Darby pause in the doorway of the tack room. A ghostly bird with lemon-drop eyes plummeted from an ohia tree and tipped its wings to Darby. She closed the tack room door and fastened it behind her in time to see the owl coast above Hoku's head, then drop over the bluff to search the pastures for a late-afternoon snack.

Francie, the fainting goat, must have seen the owl, too, because her chain jingled as she moved restlessly beside Sun House.

The owl was the family 'aumakua, a guardian rumored to be a long-dead relative, but it didn't feel mysterious to Darby anymore, nor did she take its appearance as an omen, because she saw that pueo almost every day.

"Should I buy this Oreo Leo?" Jonah asked as Darby walked back toward him.

Not knowing whether to feel flattered or unqualified to answer, Darby said, "I don't know why you need a second stallion."

"You say that because of her," Jonah said, and when he nodded at Hoku, the filly bared her teeth, "being such a tomboy?"

Darby sent her filly a mental message to be polite, even though Jonah knew very well that if Hoku hadn't run off Black Lava, the wild stallion could have injured Jonah's prized Quarter Horse stud, Kanaka Luna.

"Think while you put that on," Jonah told her, and Darby approached Hoku with the neck rope.

Because the filly was already edgy, Darby tried to remember what Jonah had told her about working in close quarters with any horse.

She shouldn't get right in front, in case the horse bolted forward. That made especially good sense when she was working with Hoku anyway. Abuse had made the filly head-shy.

"We need to mix things up a little bit," Jonah said, and when Darby glanced at him in puzzlement, he added, "With another stallion."

"If Black Lava sired some foals while he was here . . ." Darby mused as she encircled Hoku's neck with the rope.

"What?"

Jonah's roar startled Darby into dropping the rope. It fell harmlessly to the ground, but Jonah wasn't finished yelling.

"Do you have any reason to think he did?" Jonah demanded.

As Megan came sauntering into the ranch yard, a flock of small dark birds took off screeching. Darby couldn't tell if they'd been disturbed by her friend's arrival or Jonah's indignation.

"Do you?" Jonah asked again.

Darby shook her head so that the tip of her pony-tail grazed her neck.

"Not really, just that he was here, and—"

"I don't have wild horses on the place except for yours. Feel special, but do not suggest my horses interbreed with them!" Jonah held his head as if it might explode. Then, he tried to sound reasonable, breaking his sentence into distinct words. "This. Is. A. Quarter. Horse. Ranch."

He wasn't yelling anymore, but he sounded so adamant, even Hoku was studying him with intensity instead of malice.

"Your horse has shown a few moments of level-headedness," he admitted, "but don't count on it being an everyday thing."

As she walked up to see what was going on, Megan asked, "What about Tango?"

Her own wild horse was a rose roan, newly recaptured from the rain forest.

"The jury's still out on Tango," Jonah said.

"Hmph," Megan responded, then crossed her arms, taking offense on her roan's behalf.

"Put that on her," Jonah said to Darby, pointing at the fallen rope. "And tie her up closer. I want to see you do it before we get ready for our trip."

Jonah winked at Megan and she rolled her eyes in good-natured exasperation. She wasn't enthusiastic about him coming along on her school trip, but she was resigned to it.

Amused by her friend's reaction, Darby grinned for the first time since Creative Writing class. Wincing at her swim-strained muscles, she squatted to pick up the neck rope.

And then, Hoku screamed.

"Not again!" Megan wailed as the earth rocked beneath their feet.

Watching Hoku was like a nightmarish mirror, Darby thought wildly. Just as she'd once seen Joker jerk back on the hitching rack, bending his body almost double because Cade's knots held him tethered, Hoku flung herself against her lead rope, frantic to break loose, to outrun the trembling beneath her hooves.

Cade had freed the Appaloosa by cutting his neck rope, but not before Joker had damaged the hitching rack.

I thought of that! Why didn't I fix it? Why didn't I tell someone?

Darby crouched with her arms crossed over her head. Hoku's front hooves lifted. The white star on Hoku's chest rose higher.

Metal, wood, and concrete grated as Hoku

wrenched the post out of the ground on the right end of the hitching rack.

Don't let her fall over backward, Darby prayed, and then a spiral bolt or whatever it was that had fastened the hitching post to the ground pulled partway out of a gray circle and Hoku lifted it.

The post had been set in concrete. Now the rack looked like a giant hammer with a wooden handle. Hoku was the only thing keeping the hammer head of cement from crashing down on Darby's skull.

Darby closed her eyes. She hunched closer to her knees, but she didn't dare flatten herself for fear of hitting Hoku's hooves and unbalancing her.

Loud breaths and the creak of wood meant her horse was straining to hold the weight up.

Don't move, Darby told herself, and it seemed like forever before she did.

Darby was still holding her breath when Hoku's hooves struck the ground beside her.

Nothing hit her head, but what was wrong with Hoku? The sound coming from the filly wasn't equine. It sounded more like a kitten, but Darby still didn't move.

Jonah or Megan would yell when it was safe for her to stand up.

Suddenly she heard cooing, coaxing words. Megan was talking to Hoku.

No, wait, she wasn't!

"Crawl forward," Megan said in a singsong voice. "Do it now. I don't know how long we can hold it this high."

Which way was forward? And who was we? Darby opened her eyes.

She'd only scooted a few inches when Megan's moan joined Hoku's whimper.

"Go ahead and let it down," Jonah said from somewhere nearby.

On her hands and knees, Darby looked back to see Hoku straining, but Megan eased the load on the filly, supporting the rack with both arms while she coaxed Hoku to lower her head and settle the weight back to the ground.

It tipped forward, cracking off the other post. Foot-long splinters speared upward, but the rest of the rack crashed down amid the dust cloud of a felled tree.

It was only quiet for a second before Jonah apologized to Megan.

"Sorry, Mekana, but I knew if a man swooped in there, that filly—"

Megan ignored his apology.

"Can you believe that?" Megan's voice soared. "Can you? She knew she'd hurt Darby if she let it down!"

"Are you okay?" Jonah asked Megan. "And you, Darby?"

"Yeah."

"Uh-huh."

"In spite of that injury from before," Megan went on, stroking Hoku's lathered neck, "she held it up there. With the earthquake and the weight—my gosh, what do you s'pose that weighs? It's a hefty sucker, that's for sure. . . ."

Darby wondered why she didn't laugh at Megan's jabbering. She saw boots—Kimo's and Kit's—and Aunty Cathy's slippers, and heard Megan recounting what had happened.

"Darby was getting ready to put the neck rope on Hoku because she was tied by her lead rope—"

"Shoot, I did that," Aunty Cathy confessed.

"Not your fault, Mom," Megan said. "I bet when Joker got all excited during the other earthquake—the big one, remember?—he loosened the post, so it didn't take much for Hoku to jerk it out of the ground, but that's not the amazing part. Did you see, Kit?" Megan asked when the foreman made a sound of incredulity.

"Could hardly believe my eyes, but yeah. That filly figured out that thing would crash down on Darby's head if she didn't hold it up. So she did it."

"Did you see how the muscles in her neck were trembling?" Megan asked.

Darby felt boneless.

Everything around her was kind of hazy until Jonah said, "I've never seen anything like it." His tone was puzzled but reverent. "*Hapa kanaka,* that horse."

"Half man?" Darby mumbled. She blinked up at him, Megan, and Hoku.

"Thinks like a man," Jonah corrected.

"*Hapa wahine*," Darby said, substituting a Hawaiian word of her own. "My Hoku thinks like a woman."

Hoku had been standing with her legs spread wide apart. Now, watchful but weary, she lowered herself to the ground and folded her legs like a colt ready for sleep.

Even as Darby crawled to her horse, she couldn't block out the crackling of that stupid non-plagiarized paper in her borrowed sweatshirt's pocket.

It was too much, Darby thought. Her fingers worked at a knot in Hoku's flaxen mane. If only she and Hoku could crawl into a cocoon where earthquakes and suspicion didn't exist.

Jonah's voice seemed to come from another planet.

"I'd say you can take her pretty much wherever you want on the island. She can think. I'd like you to have Kit and Cade or other riders on each side of her if you're going down into Crimson Vale, but the sooner the better. You'll find out what she's made of."

Darby realized Jonah was giving permission and making plans, but her world had telescoped down to Hoku's golden tendrils and her own dirty fingernails.

". . . in shock?" Megan asked.

Darby shook her head. She just didn't want to stand up. She wanted to sit here and fill her senses with the sweet leather smell of horse hide.

Darby leaned back against Hoku's shoulder and stroked her filly's neck in gratitude.

"Granddaughter," Jonah cautioned her.

"Don't tell me not to pet her," Darby responded. "Not now. Please?"

But the suspended moment had ended.

Hoku lurched to her feet and Darby did the same. For a second, she used the horse for balance, but then Darby stood on her own and Hoku licked her neck.

Why did that make tears spring into her eyes? Darby had no idea, but they must have been extra salty, because they stung like crazy, before they burned down her cheeks.

"What?" Jonah pleaded in confusion. "I tell you she's smart, say you can ride her anywhere on the place, and—what's all this?"

Darby's sob turned into a gulp as she said, "I'm just really sick of earthquakes." She smothered a hiccup. "That's all."

Chapter Six

The next thing Darby knew, Kit was checking her arms and legs for broken bones and making her stare into his eyes to see if she had a concussion.

"Didn't we just do this?" Darby asked crankily.

"Yes, honey, but not for you," Aunty Cathy said.

"I just want to stay with Hoku," Darby said.

As Aunty Cathy led her off a few steps, Darby realized how babyish she sounded. Maybe that's why everyone was speaking to her in soothing voices.

"You can stay by Hoku," Kit said, "but if she decides to lay back down again, she doesn't need to worry about fallin' on you."

Darby nodded.

"Good"—an infuriating gulp made her sound like she'd been sobbing for hours—"point."

"Will someone please tell me what's going on?" Jonah asked.

"Wild pigs, earthquakes, volcanoes," Megan explained as she counted off on her fingers.

"No," Darby said past the catch in her voice. "It's not."

"No?" Aunty Cathy asked.

Darby shook her head.

"Well then, you'd better speak up, *keiki*," Kit said. He gave Cade a quick glance and Darby knew Cade had told Kit about Manny's threats this morning.

When the foreman turned back to Darby, he looked deadly serious.

To the others, it would probably be a letdown, Darby thought. It wasn't blackmail. It wasn't trouble on the scale that Cade faced, but it was a burden she'd never carried before. No one, especially not a teacher, had ever called her a liar.

Everyone watched as Darby reached into the sweatshirt's pocket and withdrew the papers. She unfolded them and handed the Creative Writing assignment to Jonah. She wished everyone in her ranch family wasn't looking, but it didn't really matter. Nothing stayed a secret here for long.

"That's a paper I did for my Creative Writing class."

"She wrote 'plagiarism' on it," Jonah said.

"Mrs. Martindale thought I copied this from somewhere," Darby explained, shrugging.

"She is such a witch!" Megan snapped. "Everyone knows—"

Aunty Cathy held out a hand and Megan let herself be quieted.

"'The Hawaiian,'" Jonah read the title, making Darby squirm. "It's a story?"

"Sort of. She gave us pictures and we were supposed to write descriptions," Darby rushed her words, wishing she'd never gotten into this, because Jonah's eyes darted from side to side, reading, and that was okay, but then he held the paper as if he were going to read it aloud.

"Listen to this," he said to the others. "'Haunted eyes burn from finely carved features the color of koa wood. He is robbed of language, of land, of all but his island spirit.' You wrote this?"

Dizzy with embarrassment, Darby placed a hand on Hoku's withers as if she still needed her for balance.

"Yeah," Darby admitted, "but it was a million times better inside my head. I don't know why Mrs. Martindale thought it was copied."

"Because it's really good, sis," Megan said flatly.

Darby felt her lips twist into a smile at the nickname. Megan's encouragement made her look up. Everyone else nodded in agreement and looked at her kind of expectantly.

"Okay," Darby managed. "Thanks."

"We'll go talk to her about it," Jonah said.

"She won't be at school now," Darby said. Thank goodness for that. She was grateful for everyone's support, but she didn't think Jonah would be very diplomatic in talking to her teacher.

In fact, she knew a confrontation between her grandfather and Mrs. Martindale would be a disaster.

"Come on," he said. "Let's just go see."

Darby's mouth opened, but no words came out.

"Wait, this is Victoria Martindale? Vicki, yeah?" Jonah said, glancing at Aunty Cathy, who nodded. "She's been on the island forever, lives in one of those nice houses by Hapuna Prep. I know a shortcut, won't hardly be out of our way to the airport."

Then Megan said something about luggage. Aunty Cathy and Jonah were working out a timetable for the next couple of hours. Kimo and Kit offered to do whatever was needed to fit in everything that had to be done. They were all talking at once, as if Jonah's proposition was sane.

She'd started all this, so she'd better stop it before it went any further.

"We can't go barging into her house," Darby said, gasping.

"Who said anything about barging? Give me a benefit of one doubt, Granddaughter. I have some manners," he said, joking. "I mean to knock on the door, yeah?"

"But, we can't just go to a teacher's house!" Darby told him.

"Why not?"

Darby didn't know what to say, so she held both hands out, appealing to Megan.

Megan seemed to think it over for a second, then said, "Really, Jonah . . ."

"Really, Jonah, what?"

"If we go over there on a Friday night, she might hold it against Darby," Megan said.

Jonah flapped the paper, but his voice was calm as he addressed Darby.

"Seems like she's already holding something against you. Something worse."

In the quiet, Hoku shifted nervously.

"What's that other paper, now?" Jonah asked, and Darby handed it to him. In just a few seconds, his black eyebrows flew up like bats. "From your English class?"

"Yes," Darby said. "It was an in-class essay. I thought, maybe, if I showed her that—you know, because I got an A on it and there was no chance to cheat—that she'd believe me."

"Good idea," Megan said. She joined Kimo, Cade, Kit, and Aunty Cathy as they jockeyed to look over Jonah's shoulder at the A paper. "So what did she say?"

Hoku stretched her neck, gave Darby a nudge, then lowered her head, looking for something to eat.

"I didn't show her," Darby admitted.

"Why not?" Megan asked.

"I didn't want to be pushy."

Megan moaned. Kimo shook his head. Aunty Cathy and Jonah looked at each other while Kit hung his thumbs in his pockets and squinted at Darby.

"I told her I didn't do it," Darby defended herself, but she heard how hollow that sounded.

Teachers probably got lied to all the time. A graded paper would be more like proof.

"Maybe on Monday I could try again," she said.

"Monday might never come," Kimo said.

Darby shot him a whose-side-are-you-on glare, but the cowboy just grinned.

"We're going tonight," Jonah maintained.

"Jonah, you're right," Aunty Cathy interrupted. "But that'll be cutting it awfully close. You might miss your flight."

Megan looked back and forth between the two adults. She was probably hoping Jonah would decide not to go to the airport or Oahu at all.

"It's okay, really. I'll talk to Mrs. Martindale myself," Darby said.

Jonah ignored her.

"I think we can make it. If not, there's another flight after it, one hour later, yeah?" Jonah asked.

"There is," Aunty Cathy agreed.

"Don't mean to complicate things even more," Kit

said, "but your meeting with the stud's owner is tonight."

"Really, it's okay," Darby insisted. "You shouldn't have to —"

Jonah talked right over her. "One of you call and see if we can reschedule."

"And if he can't?" Kimo asked.

Jonah shrugged. "Tell him I guess it wasn't meant to be."

"Really, it's okay," Darby said again.

"For a smart girl, you're a little slow on this. Once a bad idea worms its way into someone's brain, it's hard to get it out. Not like just washing your hands, yeah? So, which way you want her thinking about you all weekend?" He held out the two papers. "A, or cheater?"

Darby drew a deep breath and let it out, but didn't say anything.

"That's what I thought," Jonah said. "Let's get our luggage and get out of here as soon as we can," he said to Megan. "Darby Leilani, you bring along that diary of yours."

Diary? Darby's heart stopped. Her hands pounced on her hips. When she uttered random sounds of refusal, Jonah laughed.

"Just pranking you, Granddaughter. That other paper, the one from Miss Day, yeah? That will be enough to get Vicki Martindale to reconsider."

❖ ❖ ❖

Lots of girls who were paying a surprise—and unpleasant—visit to a teacher would have spent time showering, making a special effort with their hair, and changing clothes.

Instead, Darby took extra time leading Hoku to her corral. She didn't like the way the filly had folded her legs and sunk to the ground after she'd pulled the hitching rack out of the dirt.

Had she collapsed, or was she just weak from fear like Darby had been?

Darby studied Hoku's gait as she followed on a loose lead rope. Once inside the corral, with the gate closed behind them, Darby curried and massaged her horse. She paid special attention to Hoku's neck and legs.

Darby's fingers played over the filly's body, but felt no swollen muscles or tendons that were hot with strain.

Hoku just closed her eyes, enjoying the attention.

"This is a time it would be helpful if you'd let one of the guys touch you," Darby told her filly, then lowered her voice to a whisper that made Hoku's ears twitch with curiosity. "But then we might not be such good friends."

When Aunty Cathy called that it was time to leave for the airport and Mrs. Martindale's house, Darby bent at the waist and held her breath while she brushed a cloud of dust from her hair. She darted for her bedroom to change clothes.

Just as Jonah bellowed "Let's go," Darby was fastening abalone shell barrettes to keep her long hair out of her eyes.

All Darby remembered about the drive to Hapuna was that it was crowded with four of them and all the luggage. And it was very quiet.

Barbecue smoke floated around Mrs. Martindale's neighborhood. A sidewalk wound from the street, across a neat green lawn, past a table and chairs tucked in a clay-walled nook, to a screen door guarded by a black cat.

When the teacher answered Jonah's knock, she wore bright capris and a questioning smile.

"Darby Carter and . . . Jonah?" Mrs. Martindale sounded too startled for it to be a greeting. She scooped up the cat and held him under one arm as she looked between their two faces. "I see the resemblance now, but I had no idea Darby was the granddaughter of yours I'd heard about."

Mrs. Martindale left the purring cat inside as she slipped out and nodded them toward the chairs in the nook. The spot was shaded by the eaves of the house.

"I don't suppose your grandfather told you how we know each other, Darby? I didn't think so. My husband worked in Jonah's father's piggery, an eon ago," Mrs. Martindale said.

Darby made a polite sound of surprise. She'd forgotten her great-grandfather even had a piggery. She knew Jonah had told her, but she'd only remembered the fox cages.

Darby had guessed Jonah wouldn't act like this was a friendly visit, and she was right.

As soon as they were seated, he put the red-marked paper on the table and said, "Darby doesn't do that. Plagiarism. I know—" Jonah said, holding up his hand as if Mrs. Martindale had protested. "If you had a dime for every time people believed in kids that didn't deserve it—but that's not the case here. She's quite a remarkable girl, yeah?"

A current of warmth zapped through Darby. Her gruff grandfather had called her remarkable!

"From her first day in class, I liked Darby," Mrs. Martindale said, "but this isn't the writing of a student her age."

"She reads all the time," Jonah said. "She was such a bookworm, it was a problem for her back home."

It was? Darby thought.

"Even with an extraordinary grasp of language—" The teacher broke off, shaking her head.

"She's smarter than any other kid I've been around, except her mother. The actress Ellen Kealoha? You mighta heard of her. Now, Granddaughter, show Vicki the other paper."

Darby wished he wouldn't call the teacher by her first name, but she was so glad that Jonah was sitting beside her. She looked down at the in-class essay. It was a little wrinkled, so she set it on the table in front of her and smoothed it out from the center to each edge.

I couldn't have done this on my own, Darby thought. She could barely do it with her grandfather's encouragement.

"Mrs. Martindale, I just wanted to show you this paper I did in Miss Day's class. It was an in-class essay and I got a, um, pretty good grade on it." Darby glanced at Jonah. He nodded for her to go on explaining. "And I just thought that if you, uh, compared the, I don't know, like, the styles and punctuation or something, and maybe the handwriting . . ." Darby noticed Mrs. Martindale's raised eyebrows. "Yeah! No, really, I've heard that people who are copying a document change from their normal handwriting. It's subconscious, I guess, but their letters get more precise and even."

Darby stopped talking.

"Miss Day is famous for her timed essays," Mrs. Martindale said in an encouraging way.

"Uh-huh, I know," Darby said, but she was floundering. She'd been babbling eternally, and nothing had changed.

Except that Mrs. Martindale was holding her hand out.

And there was this annoying sound.

"I'd be glad to read it," Mrs. Martindale said.

The crinkling noise kept up. It was really distracting.

Darby shot a quick look around for its source and realized, with a sickening drop of her stomach: the source was her. How long had she been smoothing the paper out, over and over again, without even knowing it?

"Oh!" She jerked her hands back and looked up at Mrs. Martindale. Before she could appeal to the teacher not to believe she was always this peculiar, Mrs. Martindale slid the paper across the glass table-top and looked down at it.

While Mrs. Martindale read, Darby tried to disappear. There should be something like a reverse cocoon, she thought, so that you could shrink back into a little gray pod and be totally unnoticeable.

Mrs. Martindale arranged the essays side by side. Her eyes skimmed over them both again as she sat back in her chair, then took off her glasses and rubbed the bridge of her nose.

"This paper's from first period, Darby. Why didn't you show it to me when you talked to me after Creative Writing?"

"I'm sorry . . . " Darby began.

"No, I'm sorry," Mrs. Martindale insisted. "Jonah, Darby, I apologize to both of you. In my own defense, all I can say is that lots of kids cheat because the Internet has made it easy to snatch other people's writing."

Jonah shrugged and Darby noticed he didn't keep Mrs. Martindale on the hook like he did her or

Kimo. "Brains like hers"—he aimed a thumb at Darby and made a frustrated huff—"it's easy to misunderstand."

Mrs. Martindale returned the two papers.

"You've been very gracious. I hope next year when you're a freshman, you'll consider being on the literary magazine staff."

Darby's spirits skyrocketed. She'd just gone from being called a cheater to a student skilled enough to write for publication. Amazingly, coming here hadn't damaged her relationship with her teacher; it seemed like it was going to improve it.

"That magazine, it would be after school?" Jonah asked.

Darby felt a pang at her grandfather's question.

"Why, yes, it is, but we've received a grant for an activity bus that will take home children from outlying areas."

"I'm not sure she'll be here next year. If she's here, she'll have chores," Jonah said. He stood abruptly. "Thanks, Vicki. Tell George I said hello. I've got a plane to catch. Aloha."

"Thank you," she said, and since Jonah had already turned to go, Mrs. Martindale winked at Darby and said, "We'll work something out."

"I hope so," Darby said, holding her papers with both hands, and then hurrying after her grandfather.

As they drove to the airport, Jonah didn't say

anything about the literary magazine, but he did say, "Vicki's all right. It's easier to forgive someone for being wrong than it is when they're right and you're wrong. But Vicki won't hold a grudge. I think you can count on that."

After they dropped Jonah and Megan at the airport, amid a flurry of hugs and kisses, Aunty Cathy took Darby to a Hapuna drive-in where they both ordered huge milk shakes.

"These should keep us awake until we get back to Sun House," Aunty Cathy said, toasting Darby with her extra-large cup. "I suppose it's awful to say so, but I can't wait for a little peace and quiet this week, while those two are gone."

"It's not awful," Darby said, sipping a mouthful of cherry-chocolate milk shake. Its chocolate flakes were so big they lodged in the straw, reminding Darby she'd promised to make chocolate-chip cook-ies for Sunday's boat picnic with Ann.

They were halfway home when Aunty Cathy's favorite oldies station was interrupted by a bleating sound and an official voice. "This is an announcement from the Pan-Pacific Tsunami Center in Honolulu, Hawaii. . . ."

Aunty Cathy set her milk shake in the cup holder, turned the radio up, and tucked one side of her brown-blond hair behind her ear.

To Darby, Aunty Cathy didn't look particularly

worried that the earthquake that morning had registered 4.1 on the Richter scale and had only felt severe
because it was closer to the surface than usual.

"Is that bad?" Darby asked.

Cathy shrugged and tilted her head as the
announcement went on. "This is not a tsunami alert.
This is not a tsunami warning. Repeat, there is no
tsunami alert or warning at this time."

"At this time," Aunty Cathy echoed. "I find that
so comforting, don't you?"

Darby managed a nervous laugh. "I guess all
states have their, uh, urgent weather things," she said,
although she knew this had nothing to do with
weather. "Forest fires, landslides, floods, and hurricanes, and stuff like that."

Aunty Cathy nodded. "With all the rain we've
had, landslides and floods probably aren't out of the
question, but I think we're safe from hurricanes until
late summer. Besides, if there was a tsunami, 'Iolani
Ranch would be safe."

"Really?" Darby asked.

"Almost for sure," Aunty Cathy promised.

"But it's in a little valley," Darby said.

"True, but think of our altitude. The wave would
have to be huge to reach us. And you know what Ben
told me?"

Darby shook her head, noticing that this time
when she talked about her dead husband, Aunty
Cathy looked proud, not sad.

"Historically, tsunami come in on both sides of Night Digger Point Beach, but they never get as far inland as the ranch."

Darby visualized the island as if it were a map. 'Iolani Ranch was way uphill, but—the wild horses!

A tidal wave at Night Digger Point Beach would funnel water into Crimson Vale.

She must have looked as worried as she felt, because Aunty Cathy changed the radio station, then reached over, patted her knee, and asked, "How 'bout that Hoku?"

Darby's heart soared. Her wild filly loved her enough to save her life. Or at least her head.

"Wasn't she amazing?" Darby gushed. "I want to tell somebody who wasn't there! I'd love to tell my mother, but first I need to figure out how to put it."

"Good thinking," Aunty Cathy said with a laugh.

"Maybe I'll call Ann when we get home." Darby settled back in her seat, smiling.

"I'm not going to be using the office computer tonight," Aunty Cathy said, "if you want to e-mail one of your friends back home."

"Thanks," Darby said, but she felt a little twinge of melancholy. Would Heather, her best friend in Pacific Pinnacles, even believe her?

"*Hapa kanaka,*" Aunty Cathy said in amazement. "I've never heard Jonah say that about a horse, not even Luna."

"And he said I could ride her anywhere on the

island," Darby marveled.

"Well . . . " Aunty Cathy said cautiously.

"He did!" Darby insisted, but the radio interrupted again.

"This is a test of the Oceanic Broadcasting System. Repeat, this is just a test. Had this been a real emergency, you would have been advised to leave all low-lying areas immediately and seek higher ground. . . ."

The announcement came from a different agency than the one before. That couldn't be good.

Cathy switched off the radio. "They do those announcements after even the smallest shakes," she said. She yawned, then added, "And tonight, I'm kind of glad they do, because I can't wait to get a good night's sleep."

Chapter Seven

Hoku didn't care if she was a heroic horse.

When Darby returned to the ranch and went to see the filly, Hoku just hurried to the fence to look for hay.

"You can sniff my hands, but I haven't been anyplace that will be interesting to you," Darby told her horse. "And if you're looking for treats, I'm afraid I'll have to disappoint you."

Hoku snorted at Darby's failure to carry hay with her at all times, then wandered away.

Darby leaned against the fence, soaking up the ranch sounds of Luna neighing in his pasture, Kit strumming a guitar on the bunkhouse steps, and dogs kicking up pebbles as they skittered after each other, disputing the ownership of a stick.

Through the bunkhouse window, she saw Cade sitting at a desk, surrounded by lamplight. It was weird to see him hatless, his blond head bent over some books. Where did he get the determination to study on a Friday night? Especially given that he'd been outside working since long before dawn. And he didn't have to face a teacher on Monday morning.

Looking toward Sun House, Darby saw Aunty Cathy had switched on the lights in the kitchen before she went upstairs to her apartment.

She might be sleepy, but Darby was energized by her crazy day. It would be fun to have the whole house to herself, but first she walked to the office and settled into the padded chair, swiveled around once, then began calling Ann to tell her everything.

She was halfway through dialing when she remembered that the Potters were going to get their boat tonight.

Darby hung up.

She didn't know much about boats. This one was blue, and Ann had called it a *skiff* and said it had a canopy to act as a sun shade. Ann had laughed at her parents' efforts to research their purchase. Her mother had been reading her way through a stack of books and, after talking with local boaters, her dad had decided that even though he'd only putt along the coastline and never go out in bad weather, the skiff had to have double engines. That way, if one conked out, they wouldn't be at the mercy of the waves to either crash ashore or drift out to sea.

The only reason they were getting it was because the boys—especially Toby, the seven-year-old—had always loved boats. Ann had even promised her little brother that since they wouldn't launch the skiff until Sunday, she'd help him haul blankets and stuffed animals into the boat for a slumber party.

Now what? Darby stared from the well-lit office into the night. She could e-mail Ann, but that seemed silly, because she could call tomorrow and tell her in complete detail what Hoku had done. Having grown up in Nevada around wild horses, Ann would be almost as excited as Darby.

Darby wiggled in the chair, making it squeak as she realized no one else would appreciate the strength and intelligence it had taken for Hoku to—

No one but Samantha Forster, Darby thought suddenly.

Sam was a horse-crazy teenager who lived on River Bend Ranch in Nevada. She'd worked as a counselor for the Dream Catcher Wild Horse program Darby had joined. When a bus accident left them snowbound with an injured driver and a wounded wild horse—Hoku—Sam and Darby had become better friends than if they'd been in each other's classes all school year.

And Hoku was the full sister of a wild stallion Sam loved more than anything. Of course Sam would be excited to hear about the filly's adventures so far from her rangeland home.

She'd only e-mailed Sam once, but Darby had no trouble remembering Sam's screen name: nvcowgrrl.

That's cooler than mine, Darby thought, though her screen name, bkvandal, for "book vandal," had suited her fine when Heather, her best friend back in California, had suggested it because Darby ripped through books so fast when she read.

Darby consulted the ranch office clock and saw it was just after nine. That meant midnight in Nevada. Even though it was a Friday night, she'd bet Sam was in bed.

Still, it would be fun to write about riding Hoku, the volcano, and even about the Potters!

Darby crawled on her hands and knees, disconnecting the office telephone and plugging in the computer. There was only a dial-up connection at the ranch and, according to Aunty Cathy, they were lucky when that worked.

While Darby waited for the computer to come online, she glanced around the office. When she noticed a yellow flyer tacked on the wall, she scooted closer to read it.

Tsunami Safety!
1) Turn off utilities (electricity, gas, etc.).
2) Take route to higher ground.

3) Tsunami watch: Event may be only 1 hour away. Quakes felt under watch conditions automatically step up conditions to warning. Evacuate.
   Tsunami warning: Event may be imminent.
4) Never stand on beach to await event.
5) Once in a safe area, STAY THERE until all clear is sounded.

Darby shook her head. Who would be dumb enough to stand on the beach when a tsunami was threatening?

At last the computer was ready.

Darby had just typed in Sam's screen name and was sitting with her fingers poised above the keys, when an instant message box popped up on the screen.

nvcowgrrl: is that you, Darby?

Darby sat back in the desk chair, as surprised as if Samantha Forster had peeked into the office, right here in Hawaii.

bkvandal: it's me! why are you up so late?
nvcowgrrl: school dance—weird, huh? Prom
bkvandal: Prom?
nvcowgrrl: with Jake. His mom made him go! lol

bkvandal: I'll tell Kit! HE has a girlfriend at the feed
store!

nvcowgrrl: Perfect! Have you met her?

bkvandal: not yet—her name is ??? I hear she's an
animal rights person & vegetarian :)

nvcowgrrl: I'll try that when I go to college! My dad
would NOT be happy if I did now!

Darby sat staring at the blinking cursor. She'd
hoped Sam would be more excited about horses than
prom dresses.

And she wasn't disappointed.

nvcowgrrl: HOW IS the Phantom's little sis?!!!

bkvandal: Hoku is doing SO great! I rode her for the
first time last week!

nvcowgrrl: Yaaaaaaaaaaay!!!! How was it? Did she
buck?

bkvandal: nope, but she didn't like the sparks from the
volcano raining down on her

Sam typed an unmistakable cyber-scream. After
that, they traded quick, overlapping notes that had
Darby giggling and typing so fast she made tons of
spelling mistakes. But Sam didn't seem to care, and
by the time they both paused, Darby's cheeks ached
from smiling.

nvcowgrrl: gtg Blaze is barking because I'm rofl

Got to go and *Rolling on the floor, laughing,* Darby translated to herself.

> **nvcowgrrl:** Plus, Dallas our foreman—SO weird that Kit is yours—is helping me lunge Tempest tomorrow at 6:30. Now that will be a rodeo!!!
> **bkvandal:** tomorrow I'm riding Hoku into the rain forest to see my great-grandma and then taking the WATERFALL trail to a secret place

Darby surprised herself by typing that, but Jonah had said she could ride Hoku anyplace. And suddenly she knew why she had to go see Tutu.

> **nvcowgrrl:** sounds scary and fun!

When the soaring cliffs pocked with the burial chambers of ancient Hawaiian royalty popped into her mind, she typed another line.

> **bkvandal:** IF I keep my nerve up
> **nvcowgrrl:** you're riding a mustang so NO PROBLEM! ack my gram is coming downstairs gtg really!!!
> **bkvandal:** ALOHA!
> **nvcowgrrl:** ADIOS!
> **bkvandal:** LATER
> **nvcowgrrl:** nicker

And then Sam was gone.

Darby sat smiling, thinking she should have asked Sam how her six-month-old brother was doing. And she should have given her an update on Judge to share with Mrs. Allen.

Oh well, she'd save it all for another time. This had been way too much fun not to do again.

Darby was spinning in the office chair when a noise made her halt by grabbing the desk.

"Bart thinks you're *pupule*," Cade said from the darkness outside the office.

As Cade stepped into the light, Darby saw he was tapping his temple.

"I'm not crazy, just having fun," she told him. Then Darby called to Bart, "Hey, boy."

She smooched and the youngest of the Australian shepherds bounded in, raced around the desk, sniffed the floor where Darby had crawled to plug in the computer, then leaped onto the office couch.

When Cade and Darby laughed, the dog did it all over again, increasing his speed until he was a black-and-white blur.

"Steady." Cade used a command the Aussie was trained to obey, but Bart had already knocked over the office trash and grabbed up a ball of crumpled paper. "Down."

Bart scampered in one last circle, before flopping on his belly. Panting, he dropped the wadded paper, but kept it between his front paws.

"He's young," Cade excused the dog as it gazed

up at him with adoring eyes.

"And he doesn't have to be perfect," Darby said.

Cade made a considering sound and Darby knew he was thinking about pleasing Jonah. The dog was sort of on probation here.

"Talk about crazy, I saw you doing homework on a Friday night," Darby teased Cade.

It popped into her mind that Bart wasn't the only one Cade was trying to make perfect.

"Exams in Hapuna next week," he explained. "Earthquakes got 'em rescheduled, so I have extra time to memorize all the dates and treaties in American history. I'll be a junior if I pass."

Cade took correspondence classes specially designed for students living in remote places, and Darby admired his dedication. Without bells and teachers helping her schedule her studies, she wasn't sure she'd be a very good student—at least here on Moku Lio Hihiu.

"It's cool that you can set your own pace," Darby said. "I'd miss school, though."

"I'd miss this." Cade made a sweeping gesture that included all of 'Iolani Ranch. "Besides, I want to be a paniolo. I couldn't have a better teacher than Jonah."

"So, why are you taking all those classes? I mean, American history?" Darby asked.

"Jonah," Cade said.

Darby nodded, thinking about her grandfather's insistence that she go face Mrs. Martindale. She'd thought that was more about family honor or something than education, though.

"He promised my mom that he'd make me graduate."

Everything she'd heard about Dee, Cade's mom, contradicted the idea that she'd think a high school diploma was a big deal. People said she'd spent her life trying to be a Hawaiian hippie. She was supposed to be a big strapping woman, but she hadn't kept Manny from beating her son.

Darby's disgust must have shown on her face, because Cade said, "My mom used to be like that — like the way Jonah stood up for you — when my real dad was around. She still is inside. You should see her with that crazy pony of hers."

Darby thought that something like envy flitted across Cade's face.

"But Manny just knocked it out of her."

"Why does she stay?" Darby demanded.

"You don't know what it's like to be a single mom," Cade fired back. "That year we were alone was awful. We were starving, and — I don't remember it, but I guess getting hit is better than being hungry."

"I guess," Darby agreed, but she only said that for Cade. She didn't point out that her parents weren't together, or that she'd rather be hungry any day than live with someone like Manny.

Why couldn't Manny just leave the island? He'd caused most of the trouble around here. At least the trouble that wasn't caused by nature. And nature's crises were easier to take, because they'd happen whether humans were around or not.

Manny meant to be mean.

That girl's like a monkey, he'd said about her, and he would have said it to her face, too.

Manny didn't trust her because there was "too much" going on in her head.

Good! She'd take that as a compliment and hope he kept his distance.

But what about Joker? Would Manny use some phony document to take the Appaloosa away unless Cade paid him off with the reward money?

She swallowed hard. She wanted to ask Cade what he thought, but when she started to, Darby noticed the torment had left Cade's features. Obviously, he wasn't thinking about Dee and Manny anymore.

"Hey, if you want to take Hoku out, like Jonah said, me 'n' Kit worked it out with Kimo," Cade offered. "So we could go with you."

"Tomorrow?" Darby asked.

"Only if you want," he said kindly. "No pressure."

For some reason, though, Darby remembered Jonah going on about her horse while she was still sitting, in shock, next to the ruined hitching rack.

He'd said something about seeing what Hoku was made of.

Then, she'd barely heard him, but now she felt

proud. She knew exactly what Hoku was made of. Half mustang, half Quarter Horse, and all heart.

Darby was nodding to herself, thinking how clever she could have sounded if she'd been thinking straight, when she heard the silken rustle of wings. It must be the *pueo*.

"Thanks," she said to Cade. "Let's do it. Go on the ride."

Darby knew she sounded distracted, but the owl was making himself known again and this time it was no gentle reminder. Wings, impact, a shrill cry, and then a clicking sound.

A beak on bones? Darby thought, recoiling as Bart growled.

"Just an owl huntin'," Cade soothed the dog.

"Tomorrow I've got to go see my tutu before I ride anywhere else."

"Is everything okay?" Cade asked.

"Sure," Darby said.

With his hair scraped back in a braid, it was easy to see the frown line between Cade's eyebrows. He didn't believe her.

So Darby tried to distract him with a chattering account of her meeting with Mrs. Martindale. It took a while, but she kept talking until he lost that watchful look, until Bart fell asleep and Cade's eyes had glazed over with boredom. Then she stopped and gave a yawn that was only half fake.

"Come down to the tack shed when you're ready t'go," Cade said.

"I will," Darby promised, and as she watched Cade and Bart walk away, she was glad she'd been able to keep her secret a little longer.

Cade knew about the *lei niho palaoa*, the ancient necklace she'd found weeks ago. He and Megan had been the ones who'd told her that the necklace, made from the hair of royalty, was either cursed or sacred, depending on who held it.

Darby had hidden the necklace in the cave behind the Shining Stallion waterfall. She'd thought it would be safe there. But what if the necklace wasn't at home?

She didn't make fun of herself for that thought.

Hawaii held many mysteries.

Darby swallowed hard as she peered into the darkness between the office and the porch lamp of Sun House.

Cade wouldn't mock her for wondering if all of the near-miss disasters she'd faced were her ancestors trying to tell her something.

Still, she wanted to talk this over with Tutu first. Her great-grandmother was a wise woman when it came to herbs, history, and human nature.

In fact, Tutu might point to the trail of calamity — a rabid pig, earthquakes, and a volcanic eruption — behind Darby and ask why it had taken her great-granddaughter so long to realize the spirits were trying to get her attention.

Darby switched off the office lights, took a deep breath, and sprinted for home, trying to recall why it had seemed so appealing to have the whole empty house to herself.

 Chapter Eight

The next morning, Darby woke to an unnaturally quiet Sun House.

Even though there was little chance of disturbing Aunty Cathy, Darby found herself tiptoeing around to get ready. Aunty Cathy deserved to sleep in. Besides, she was thirteen years old. She could certainly get herself fed and ready for the ride, and she already had Jonah's permission to go.

Because the weather had been so unpredictable, Darby layered a long-sleeved pink shirt over her pink tank top and tied a blue bandanna around her neck. Jonah had showed her how to wet it with water from a canteen, then sponge off Navigator's neck, or stand up in her stirrups and squeeze water between his ears if he overheated.

She'd spotted Megan's old maroon boots, the ones she'd wear today, by the bench in the entrance hall, so she padded out of her bedroom in her socks.

Standing in the kitchen, munching a handful of granola, she was determined to do whatever Tutu told her about the necklace. She was pretty sure her great-grandmother would tell her to retrieve the ancient treasure and turn it over to a museum or a Hawaiian elder.

Either action was fine with her. In fact, it was better than fine. She already felt satisfied that Tutu's decision would be right.

Darby wrote a note telling Aunty Cathy that she, Cade, and Kit were riding into Crimson Vale and would be back before dark. They'd probably get back earlier, but that would keep Aunty Cathy from worrying. And Aunty Cathy was a big worrier.

Darby tried not to be. She was getting braver. Last night, for instance, she hadn't had nightmares about dark-draped chanting ladies or tsunamis. But she had stayed awake wondering how was she supposed to tack up Hoku. The filly had never felt the touch of a saddle or bridle.

As Darby left Sun House, she thought how lucky she was to be surrounded by experts. She only had to get herself ready for this ride. Kit and Cade would pack saddlebags and even slickers if they thought they'd need them. And, once she reached the tack room, she'd ask Kit or Cade for advice on tack for Hoku.

Darby's instincts told her to do what Hoku was used to, but "used to" was stretching it. She'd only ridden her filly once, in the lava tube, and that time she'd ridden bareback, with only a halter and lead rope for guidance.

Joker was tied to a ring on the tack room wall. In quick, short strokes, Cade groomed the Appaloosa's gray coat splattered with black spots. He held the gelding's sparse black tail and brushed out its few snarls, then turned his attention to hooves that were faintly striped gray and white.

When Darby thought of the two running away from an abusive home together, it was no wonder Joker would do anything for Cade.

Cade barely looked at Darby, merely raising his hand. Could he be embarrassed because he'd been so open, talking about his mother last night?

Just then, Kit shouted from the bunkhouse porch, "Cade, ya gotta see this."

Responding to the urgency in Kit's voice, Cade tossed the dandy brush toward a basket, then bolted around the side of the building. He was already up the stairs when Darby rounded the corner after him. Hearing the television turned up loud, she looked up at Kit and asked, "Tsunami warning?"

Kit shook his head.

"Mornin', Darby," he said. "C'mon in."

The house smelled like coffee and bacon, and the

TV, which was smaller than most microwave ovens, blared.

"Look at that." Cade spoke so quietly, Darby knew he was addressing himself.

The screen showed vines and greenery swarming over a damaged house as the newscaster's smooth voice began, "The first April earthquake shook Manuel Billfish's house off its foundation—"

"That's not his last name!" Cade snapped.

". . . slamming his wife into the door, leaving her with injuries that still show." The newscaster was still off-screen, but the camera lingered for a few seconds on the bruised face of a woman with limp blond hair.

"Yeah, right," Cade grumbled. "Do you believe this guy?"

"This guy" was Manny. Even though he wore a blue-and-white shirt over his usually bare chest, Darby recognized Cade's stepfather. But what was he doing on television?

Then the camera followed the reporter on a brief tour. Darby recognized him as the one who'd interviewed Babe when Stormbird disappeared, the one Babe had said liked horses. Mark somebody.

"Everything in the house, including light fixtures, is still on the floor." The reporter pointed out a dented metal lamp base, shattered dishes, and wires dangling on the front porch.

Darby recalled how fast the broken dishes had been cleared away at 'Iolani Ranch. Despite Aunty

Cathy's concussion, she and Megan had set to work throwing out things that couldn't be saved, then sweeping up crumbs and broken glass. At the same time, Darby had been seeing to the horses, Cade had been checking the cattle, and Kit had set to work making outdoor repairs.

And yet the woman who must be Dee, Cade's mother, still sounded shaken.

"Every time we put things up, they get jiggled back down," she said.

The camera focused on Manny as he kicked at a buckled board on the porch.

"Even if I had the money to pay, I couldn't get anyone out here to help me rebuild. Most construction guys, yeah? They have all the work they want without driving down that road."

Manny gave a dismal laugh as the television screen showed the almost vertical dirt road that Darby remembered from her first day on the island.

"But Manny and Dee haven't given up," the reporter went on.

Gag me. That's what Megan would say if she were here, but Darby kept quiet and wondered how the horse-loving reporter would feel if he knew the truth about Manny.

"I'm waiting for an investment to pay off so I can do the repairs myself," Manny said.

Darby glanced at Cade. Was he thinking what she was? That Manny's "investment" was the reward money he was trying to extort from Cade?

"Thousands of dollars' worth of damage to his dwelling and outbuildings," the reporter said sympathetically, "and now this."

"This" was a photographic shot of plants squashed in a swamp.

Before Darby could turn to Cade or Kit for an explanation, the reporter went on. "The island's storied wild horses have been joined by two animals belonging to Billfish. Possibly disturbed by the earthquakes themselves, the horses have overrun the farmer's taro field, trampling what they can't eat."

"The farmer," Cade muttered ironically.

"That's Black Lava and—" Darby gasped, pointing at the shot of two horses onscreen.

"My steeldust mare!" Kit shouted.

The camera zoomed in enough that they could clearly see the black stallion and his silver-and-black mare, the heavy-maned horse Darby had glimpsed and thought of as Medusa.

"Those 'two animals' don't belong to him," Darby said.

But now Manny's face filled the TV screen once more.

"As soon as I catch them, those two are going to the highest bidder. I hate to part with 'em, but I've got to patch my roof."

"Those aren't his horses!" Darby yelled, wishing the reporter could hear.

The television showed water dripping into a pot that was set on the cluttered floor, with the reporter's voice-over saying, "From the Billfish house near Crimson Vale, Moku Lio Hihiu, I'm Mark Larson."

"Your steeldust mare?" Cade asked, and Darby thought that Kit's claim must have really surprised Cade if that's what his mind clung to out of all the lies and half truths in the report.

Kit took his time untying, then retying, his leather string necklace studded with brown-streaked turquoise stones. Then he cocked his head toward Darby. "Well, you remember I told you I might want to train me a wild horse."

"You said you'd seen one that reminded you of Jake's mare, Witch, right?" Darby asked.

"She's the one," he said, pointing to the television. "Black Lava's lead mare. What d'you think the chances are of her workin' into a nice, well-behaved cow pony?" He snorted at his own foolishness.

"I don't know," Cade said. "You're awful good with horses."

Kit shrugged off Cade's praise as Darby added, "And look at Hoku."

"Anyway, you have just as much right to her as anyone else," Cade added. "She's not Manny's horse and neither is Black Lava. Moku Lio Hihiu's wild horses belong to the island and there's a conservancy, whatever that is, that watches over 'em." Cade slumped against the wall thinking for a few minutes, but then his face contorted in anger and he stood with his hands on his hips and turned to Kit. "Do you believe that?"

"No, but I believe I'll call Mark Larson and tell him how many lies he's been fed," Darby said, and she'd absolutely do it. If Mark Larson liked horses enough to film Babe's appeal for Stormbird and do a story about riding on the beach, he deserved to know the truth about Manny.

"And I believe," Kit put in, "that I know just where we're gonna be riding today."

For a second Darby thought she glimpsed what Sam had called Kit's "happy wolf" grin, but then she decided she was wrong.

The Nevada cowboy looked more like a man who couldn't wait to settle a score.

Hoku wasn't happy, either.

The filly didn't mind that Darby had hurried her through her breakfast. She didn't protest when Darby eased onto her back after fastening the halter rope in one continuous rein. Hoku even welcomed the company of Navigator and Joker—but being flanked by two human males? That was simply too much.

"It's okay, girl," Darby said, but Hoku's chest expanded with deep breaths. Trapped between Kit and Cade, she ignored Darby's voice, legs, and the hands that held the rope rein so softly.

Darby tried to read her filly's emotions, but Hoku's attitude seesawed between dread and a spirited insistence that she could just bolt and be rid of them all.

"Don't let her feel one tick of worry. Leak all your air out and settle into her back." Kit sounded almost sleepy as he watched Darby.

Darby leaned back a little and relaxed her legs, and suddenly her tailbone didn't grate on Hoku's backbone. She smiled to let Kit know he'd helped her make a big improvement.

"That's it. Now, just make your neck and shoulders mush, and melt on into her."

Darby tried, and instantly felt Hoku's tight muscles loosen. Her twitching tendons eased, too. As she hummed to the filly, Darby felt her own eyelids droop.

Much better, she thought, and they'd only walked as far as Sun House.

Hoku snorted when Aunty Cathy pattered barefoot down the stairs from her apartment, holding her camera.

"Wait, I want to take a picture of Darby and Hoku," she said to Kit. Then she added, "Don't you think your mom would like a photo of you two on your first real ride? It'll show her how far you've come."

"Yeah," Darby said it quietly, but she felt a burst of gladness. Aunty Cathy must know she wanted to live here for good, and she was helping her bring her mother around to her way of thinking.

While Cathy focused, Hoku stood quietly, eyes fixed on a bird in the candlenut tree. But the door to the upstairs apartment hadn't completely closed, and Pip, a tiny white terrier, shot down the stairs and planted herself, yapping, among the horses.

Navigator snorted. Joker squealed and threw his head as high as his reins allowed.

Hoku hadn't forgotten Pip's teasing forays under her corral fence and out again. Darby felt the filly gathering for payback. Even as Darby shortened her rope rein, Hoku's neck arched in an openmouthed threat, and then she struck out with a forefoot.

It was warning enough for the little dog. Pip whirled, sprinted back up the stairs, and stood barking from there.

"Got it!" Aunty Cathy said, laughing. "You have fun now. And come back right away if there's another earthquake," she added. "Or anything."

The three had been riding for about half an hour when Kit said, "Before we go see your tutu, what if we make a little detour out to—what did that reporter fella call it?" Kit put on a really annoying Western accent. "The Fishbill estate?"

"Billfish," Cade corrected with a chuckle.

"Could we go by Tutu's first? I won't take long. I promise," Darby told the foreman.

She didn't want to frustrate him, but if Tutu told

her to get the necklace, they'd be right there, sort of in the neighborhood.

Besides, both Cade and Kit were so irritated by Manny's lies, it probably wouldn't hurt them to cool down for an extra half hour.

Or a bit more, Darby thought. Hoku's head was swinging from side to side and her nostrils flared wide, testing the air.

The only time the filly had come this way outside a trailer, she'd been running away. Darby tightened one hand and then the other on the rein, distracting the filly. She didn't want Hoku to recall the smell of freedom.

Almost as if she'd known they were coming, Tutu rode Prettypaint out to meet them exactly where they would have turned onto a rain-forest path to her cottage.

And that meant Darby had a problem. How could she have a private talk with Tutu about the necklace, if they were all four together at this crossroads in the forest?

This wasn't the first time Tutu had done this, and Darby would have believed her great-grandmother really was psychic, if Tutu hadn't said she simply read the birds' reactions to approaching humans.

"Aloha." Tutu greeted Darby in that voice that seemed too hearty for her slender form. Tutu's gaze met and held the eyes of each of them. It seemed like the old woman weighed their hearts' heaviness and took it all on herself.

Where did that come from? Darby asked herself. Something about Hawaii brought out mystical notions in her brain, and she wasn't sure she liked it.

Darby shook her head and shifted her attention to Prettypaint.

The blue-and-white horse, not quite a paint or an Appaloosa, didn't flash her ears to warn Hoku away. She flowed alongside the sorrel and the two matched steps as if they'd known each other forever.

At last, Tutu said, "Going down into Crimson Vale, by Shining Stallion Falls—you're not, are you?"

It was exactly the destination Darby had been picturing.

She'd never heard her great-grandmother's voice quaver and sound unsure before.

"No, we were thinking of seein' the valley from the rainbow trail, then head downhill past the lily ponds, on toward the taro fields," Kit said. "Just taking Hoku for an outing."

"*Shouldn't* we go into Crimson Vale?" Darby asked.

"There's no official tsunami warning," Cade told Tutu.

"Nope, I had the TV on this morning," Kit assured her. "Didn't say nothin' about one."

Tutu nodded seriously. "Just be careful and listen. Although"—she gave a humorless laugh—"by the time you hear one, it's too late."

Darby shuddered and Hoku sidestepped, bumping shoulders with Prettypaint.

Get a grip, Darby told herself. Neither Kit nor Cade would knowingly take her into danger.

"No, if I were you, I wouldn't go down in the valley itself," Tutu said. "I was trapped there once, and though I look back on the experience with warmth now, we were fortunate to survive."

"You were trapped there by a tsunami?" Cade asked, and Darby realized she wasn't the only one this story was new to.

"Maybe," Tutu said. "Those who study such things say there hasn't been a significant tsunami for a hundred years."

"That's when stories about the tsunami horses started, right?" Cade waited for Tutu's nod, then turned to Kit and Darby. "There was a warning, and the farmers—real farmers," he clarified, "knew they didn't have time to get their stock up the hill and out of Crimson Vale, so they just turned all of them loose. Some escaped and turned wild."

"Most of those that survived made it to the *kipuka.*" Tutu paused. She glanced at Darby to make sure she remembered the word.

Of course she did. She'd spent several nights on one—a rain-forested spot like an oasis, surrounded by a field of lava rock.

"Which *kipuka*?" Kit asked.

"It's been under water for years now, but it was

out by Crescent Cove," Tutu said. "You know where that finger of black rock seems to point into the sea?"

They all nodded.

"But most of the horses drowned," Cade insisted.

Darby glared at him. He sounded like a little boy, loving the gory parts of a story. And then he made it even worse by holding one hand up, cupping his ear to listen to a far-off sound.

Melodramatically, he said, "And sometimes at night, you still hear their panicky hooves running, searching for safety before they were swept away . . . "

Kit laughed at Cade's creepy tone, but Darby didn't. She remembered the night she'd sensed a horse beneath the candlenut tree outside her window. Kimo had suggested it had been the ghost of a tsunami horse.

Tutu gave a faraway smile. "I never saw the tsunami, just a towering wet shadow looming over us, then pulling back."

"What happened then?" Darby asked. She inched forward on Hoku's back without meaning to, and the filly shied sideways.

Grabbing a handful of mane along with the rein, Darby managed to stay on, but her heart thundered so hard, she barely heard Tutu suggest they all dismount for a few minutes.

They sat on a log, listening as Tutu began her story.

"I'd gone alone to Crimson Vale to check on the

horses our family grazed in the valley," Tutu explained. Her voice was so soothing, Hoku sneezed, shook her mane, and when she looked at Darby again, the wildness had left her eyes.

"We'd had a series of earthquakes, and one of my favorite mares was in foal," Tutu said. "I had to make sure she was all right, even though my husband—Jonah's father—didn't want me to go. You see, I was near my own time to give birth.

"But I insisted. Strangely, when I got there, most of the horses were gone, but not my mare. Another earthquake struck, and my saddle horse escaped. I couldn't go after him, because Jonah had decided to be born. He came into the world safely, but then a tidal wave—a tsunami—struck with the power of a volcano.

"I was holding Jonah to my heart, looking over his head toward Night Digger Point Beach and a massive brown crest"—Tutu curved her hand like a hook—"showed for an instant, then vanished.

"We made it into a cave and the horses followed, before cliffs collapsed and trails washed out. I always wondered if the other horses fled the valley because of some instinct left from that century-past tsunami, but the four of us couldn't follow.

"We were tucked away, safe—the mare, foal, Jonah, and I—for two weeks."

"Weren't they looking for you?" Darby asked.

"Of course, but the roads were blocked with mud

and uprooted trees. Landmarks had washed away
and it was hard to tell if you were going where you
meant to. In fact, it was rather like one of those fun
houses at a carnival, where you enter a room with the
furniture nailed to the ceiling. It's just hard to get
your bearings."

Darby wondered when Tutu had been to a carnival, and where? She seemed so much a part of the
tropical rain forest, it was hard to picture her anyplace else.

"Finally, I quit waiting to be found. I rode the
mare out, carrying Jonah in a sling made from the
hem of my dress. The foal followed and, within an
hour, we crossed paths with the search party, just as
if it had been fated."

"Just the same, we won't count on fate," Kit said.
He didn't sound rude, but his voice was firm.

"No, I wouldn't," Tutu said. "Those were the old
days, when such things happened. Today? Perhaps
we've insulted Mother Earth so often, we'd be fools
to depend on her mercy."

With Tutu's story at an end, Darby saw her
chance to ask her great-grandmother about the necklace, but something kept her from doing it in front of
Kit and Cade.

"Excuse me, ladies, but broncs have left me with
a lifetime supply of stiff legs. I'm going to stretch 'em
a little before I get back in the saddle," Kit said. He
made a clucking sound to Navigator. "C'mon, big

boy. I hear a stream. Let's get you a drink of water."

Perfect, Darby thought. Now if only Cade would go with him.

"Cade, why don't you come, too?" Kit asked.

"I'm okay." Cade sounded content to stay seated on the log with Darby and Tutu.

"Cade," Kit repeated, "bring Joker along to the stream."

So it wasn't a coincidence, Darby thought. Kit knew she wanted time alone with Tutu.

Cade blushed, ducked his head, and left the females together.

Chapter Nine

Darby stalled. She lifted the soft rope rein over Hoku's head so that the filly could graze behind the log. She took a deep breath, preparing to confess she might have made a serious mistake. Then, as soon as the cowboys left the clearing, she blurted out the story of the sacred necklace.

She told Tutu how the braided hair and shell ornament had snagged on her jeans, then made the journey with her through the waters off Night Digger Point Beach, and back home to 'Iolani Ranch. She explained that Cade and Megan had told her of the necklace's significance, warned her of its power, and helped her keep it safe from Manny, who sold Hawaii's treasures on the black market.

"Sit," Tutu said, patting the log beside her, and Darby realized she was still standing behind the log and she'd confessed everything to the sleek knot of silver hair on the back of her great-grandmother's head.

Darby sat, but when she turned to see Tutu's expression, the old woman said, "Jonah tells me you hid the necklace instead of waiting for Uncle Kindy." It took Darby a moment to remember the name. "Uncle" was an honorary name for a respected elder, this time. Not another surprise relative.

"I—Jonah told you?" Darby asked, but of course he had!

Even though Jonah and Tutu had a hot-and-cold relationship, this was important. Darby had taken the fate of the necklace into her own hands instead of waiting for a Hawaiian elder to do what was right.

"You told it better," Tutu said, taking Darby's hand between both of hers. "And he didn't judge your decision."

"But I should have waited for Uncle Kindy." Darby knew she didn't say it with much conviction. She'd never met the man. To be honest, she was a little afraid to meet him.

"Did you treat the necklace with respect?" Tutu asked.

"I think so. I tried to," Darby said. "I hid it in the cave behind Shining Stallion Falls and there were—well, I didn't look closely because it seemed like an intrusion—but there were . . ."

Tutu released Darby's hand so she could cross her arms over her chest, fingertips touching each shoulder in the position she'd glimpsed, or imagined she noticed the shapes of ancient figures in the cave.

Darby nodded and said, "I thought the necklace belonged with them."

"It might have. Or they might have been guardians," Tutu said. "The *ali'i*, the royal ones, could be in burial chambers in the cliffs or in one of hundreds of lava tubes, or in a chamber disguised by a rock wall, one we'll never find."

"So, did I make a terrible mistake? Do you think all of this . . ." Darby tried to make a wide gesture that would take in the volcanoes and the sea, but Tutu's powdery soft grip had claimed her hands again. For an old lady, she held on tight. Darby sighed and finished, "Is all this turmoil because of what I did?"

"What do you think?" Tutu asked with maddening patience.

"I don't know! It's like the old religion and culture—today's culture—and laws are all mixed up together. Half of me thinks that necklace belongs in a museum. Then, everyone can appreciate our history and learn from it. And it would be protected from grave robbers like Manny!

"But when Jonah tells me that he'll never sell the ranch—that the soil's powdered with the bones of his ancestors—" Darby broke off, seeing Jonah's passionate face in her memory. "That he'll grab the bulldozers' blades with his bare hands before he lets them be disturbed—that means something to me."

For a moment, Darby only heard Hoku nosing into a shrub, and the clip of the filly's teeth as she investigated its taste.

At last Tutu said, "It's an old question: Who speaks for the ancestors?"

Can't you do it? Darby thought, but Tutu's expression was distant, as if this conversation had ended.

"So what should I do?" Darby asked just as her hand grabbed tighter on the rope rein.

Hoku's head lifted and she nickered. Maybe Cade and Kit were coming back with the other horses.

"Only you can decide," Tutu told her.

Darby wanted to decide right now. The necklace had already been in limbo long enough. "I want to get it, then give it to Uncle Kindy— No. I want to give it to you."

"Just to be rid of it and have it off your conscience?" Tutu asked.

Was that it? As Darby turned the question over in her mind, she saw sunlight sifting through the rainforest canopy. Warmth wrapped around her. She thought of a bug suspended in amber. It was nice, sitting here in silence, but if she didn't answer, Tutu might think she was too immature to have an opinion.

"No, I want to give it to you because I think you'll

know best what to do with it," she told her great-grandmother.

Tutu looked pleased. She pulled her pink cloak up on her shoulders and raised her silver eyebrows. "That may be best," she said, "but not now. Crimson Vale isn't safe. Wait until the present danger, this storm shadow, has passed on."

A pulse of panic thumped through Darby. "But maybe then it will be too late. Maybe the tsunami or flood won't come if the necklace gets to its proper place now."

Tutu laughed.

It's not funny, Darby thought, shocked by her great-grandmother's reaction.

"We've come a long way since the days of human sacrifice, Darby Leilani. No one will die because the necklace remains in the safekeeping of that blue-eyed stallion for a few more days."

Darby was dissatisfied by her agreement to stay away from Crimson Vale, but Kit and Cade were happy. Even though they'd have to travel a roundabout way to Cade's old home, they were itching for a confrontation with Manny.

"This is takin' too long," Cade grumbled, but he lifted one shoulder in a shrug that indicated he knew they had no choice.

"We'll eat in the saddle," Kit said. "If anyone's hungry."

They'd spent more than an hour with Tutu, and after they'd left the rain forest, the three riders had to travel cross-country before taking a steep trail to higher ground.

Darby was hungry, and it was well past lunchtime, but when the trail descended and turned wet, there was no way she'd let herself be distracted by eating. She had to keep all of her attention on her horse and the path they were riding.

Lehua blossoms had been tramped into the mud. Cade and Kit both mumbled that they'd noticed, too, and kept riding.

Horses had clearly come through this way ahead of them, Darby thought, and she doubted they were domestic horses. There were too many of them.

As the trail climbed again, she kept her mind on wild horses and red flowers, which were sacred to Pele, instead of her growling stomach.

Darby knew the blossoms had been hammered off the trees by wind and rain, but her mind brimmed with stories of the two goddess sisters, fighting battles with waves and lava.

And it was raining again. Rivulets of water twisted over earth that was too saturated to soak up another drop.

Despite the hoofprints, Navigator and Joker gave no signs that wild horses were nearby, and Hoku took on much of her trail mates' calmness. For a while.

She was still young, and a newcomer to this place, and when they rode through a tunnel of greenery, Hoku's ears swiveled and she turned anxious, distracting Darby from her growling stomach.

At first she thought the filly was reacting to the sounds of waves she couldn't see, as they struck the rocks below.

Darby was coaxing her horse to look between the trees and vines to catch glimpses of the sea, when Hoku lowered her head to sniff at the trail.

There, stamped into the mud, was the hoofprint of Black Lava. The powerful black stallion with one brown eye and one sapphire eye had been marked on the day he escaped from Jonah. A line had been cut in his hoof so that her grandfather could identify the stallion if he returned to the ranch.

He'd passed this way, and his scent made the filly uneasy. She stayed tense until they emerged into the sunlight where rainbows shimmered on a waterfall.

With an inquiring nicker, Hoku watched hissing silver drops arch over the trail. After inspecting the brilliant thing, Hoku ducked under the arc of water and followed Navigator's coarse black tail.

"Look at that," Cade said suddenly.

"Can't say I want to," Kit replied.

Darby glanced to her left. From here, the rows of emerald-green plants below looked ruler straight.

"This way," Cade said, nodding in the other direction, toward the ocean side.

At first Darby only saw the ragged trail edge. Rain runoff had taken bites from it. If Hoku took just one step too many, the muddy edge might give beneath her hooves and they'd plummet thousands of feet down.

Even though rain coursed through Darby's hair and down her neck, she made no move to stop it. She kept both hands closed on the rope rein.

Then she realized Cade was pointing farther out to sea, at the black lava spit.

She and Hoku had actually swum around it once, escaping high tide in the crescent-shaped cove. But the spit looked different now, and Cade was trying to figure out why.

"When the tide's high, it looks like a bunch of boulders, and the wave just comes in around them. When the tide's low, it looks like a sea serpent with humps of back poking up, but—" Cade broke off, shaking his head, and Darby remembered that Cade's childhood had been spent on this island coastline. "I've never seen it so exposed," he finished.

It looked like a single formation, Darby thought. She'd seen molten lava stream into the ocean, then start to cool and harden. This lava stream looked like a black finger slipping into the water to touch something round.

"It's the *kipuka* Tutu talked about," Darby said in astonishment. "It's there again."

"She said it was underwater," Cade replied.

"Shoot," Kit said, "I thought it was just part of that tsunami horse legend."

"Why does it look like it's moving?" Darby wished for a pair of binoculars. "Is it covered with ferns or something?"

Cade rose in his stirrups for a better view. "Could be birds. It's so far off, I can't tell."

Kit's quiet exclamation stopped their conversation.

Motionless, Darby strained her senses. At last she heard hooves, but she couldn't tell where the sound was coming from, and she couldn't risk shifting around on Hoku's bare back.

All at once she felt vulnerable. On this high trail, with no helmet or seat belt, no modern precaution at all, she could only depend on her horse to keep her safe—her wild, untrained young horse.

Hoku whinnied, and Navigator joined in. Joker swung his hindquarters and stepped back. A clump of the trail edge broke off and splattered on the rocks below.

Darby leaned forward. She pressed each palm against the rope where it lay on Hoku's shoulders. She willed calm to flow from her into the wary mustang.

Don't pay attention to Joker. Stay with me, she told Hoku silently.

"Easy," Cade said, then walked the Appaloosa past the others, keeping him in forward motion.

Wild horses, led by Black Lava, had passed this stretch of trail.

She hoped no more were behind them. If another horse crowded onto this trail, it would turn into a death trap. There wasn't much choice between pitching toward the ocean or down the rock face to the valley floor.

A whine sung over the far-off thud of hooves.

"Gunshot," Kit grumbled.

Just what we need, Darby thought. She kept stroking Hoku's mane and murmuring wordlessly, but Darby's mind raced to fit the sights and sounds together.

A tan house sat on a hillside overlooking the emerald-green plants she'd seen before. Manny's taro field, Darby thought, was in a gully bordered by earthen walls. And those swift darts of brown, black, and cream, cutting through the green in the distance, must be wild horses.

But why was he firing his rifle?

"He said he wanted to catch them!" Darby tried to keep her voice low and serene, but it was impossible.

"He wanted the steeldust and stallion. That's all," Cade said. Ahead of the others, he set Joker on a quicker pace. "Let's get down there."

"Hurry!" Darby called.

"Naw, take it easy," Kit told Cade.

With a quick nod, Cade signaled that he knew Kit

was right. The young paniolo kept Joker at a walk, but Darby could tell he didn't like it.

"But—" Darby cut off her protest.

You're just a city girl, she reminded herself. She had to trust the judgment of these two expert horsemen.

But Manny's shots could hit Black Lava or a member of his band. Hadn't he ever heard of ricochets? Or accidents? And the black stallion was fierce. Darby had seen him charge.

He might do it. And Manny might stop him with a bullet.

But my job, Darby told herself, *is to keep Hoku calm.*

Darby had ended up riding last in line, contrary to Jonah's orders, so Kit glanced back at her as he spoke.

"Now, a man's entitled to defend his crop. I'm a rancher, so I understand. But there's a hundred ways to run off those horses without gunfire. As for hurrying, we're too far away to stop him, if killing's what he has in mind."

You have a rifle. Darby almost said it out loud, but then she noticed the horses weren't eating Manny's crop.

"They're not grazing in the taro," Darby said suddenly.

Closer, it was easy to see that the horses weren't pausing at all. They were taking the easiest path to the beach.

A bay mare waited at the bottom, looking up at a

black foal. The last of the herd and the youngest, the foal's legs shook from exhaustion. He feared the short leap that would land him just steps from his mother.

The mare glanced over her shoulder at the rest of the mustangs. They trotted through the taro fields. A few grabbed leaves in passing, but none stopped. They were headed toward the sun diamonds, glinting on the teal-blue sea.

Why had they left Crimson Vale? Had something told them their home was no longer safe?

Cade and Joker were just behind the foal now, and their presence goaded the foal into a jump. He lurched off the trail and landed raggedly beside his mother. He tried to nurse in relief, but the mare nosed him after the others, and the foal staggered on.

The cove was a beautiful destination, but why would the horses leave the grass and safety of Crimson Vale for a barren beach? Why brave the presence of humans and gunshots, when they had a cove of their own bordering Crimson Vale?

It didn't make sense.

Squish-squash hoof falls from the mare and foal ended as the pair clambered up and over the basin around the taro patch. They were the last ones. All the horses Darby could see had made it to the beach.

And Manny's bullets hadn't taken a single one.

"What are they doing?" she asked Cade.

When Cade pulled Joker to a stop, Kit reined Navigator around the Appaloosa, then set his heels to the Quarter Horse.

Mud flew up from Navigator's huge hooves as he broke from a walk to a jog.

Kit planned to reach Manny before Cade did.

Cade didn't race him for it. He took his hat off as if he could see better and understand more without it.

"There are sharks out there, and dangerous currents, and they know it." Cade sounded puzzled as he squinted past the falling rain.

The horses weren't running blindly. They were not playing a deadly game of follow the leader. They had left their valley, taken a shortcut through Manny's fields, and now they were splashing, walking, and swimming for the end of the lava spit.

The *kipuka* had kept horses safe from a tsunami a hundred years ago. If the wild horses were driven by some ancestral memory, they couldn't know that the knob of land and lava sat much lower in the water now.

"From here, where's Night Digger Point Beach?" Darby's mouth had gone so dry, she croaked the words.

Cade turned in the saddle and pointed.

"Kinda east, southeast, I—"

Cade broke off and he must have been looking in the same direction she was, because he said, "There's nothing, see? And no guarantee, even if there was one coming, that it would make land from the same direction."

And yet she noticed Cade couldn't even make himself say the word *tsunami*.

Darby knew that tsunamis started as tiny ripples on the sea floor, then pulled back millions of gallons of ocean water to build a wave. She'd read it was like a person removing a carpet, not by rolling it up neatly, but pulling at the edge of a rug. You'd pull and tug until the floor was gradually uncovered, then totally bare, and the carpet curled in a heavy, ungainly mass that finally tipped you facedown with its weight.

A tsunami could be building now.

She didn't hear anything, but Tutu had said once you did, it was too late.

Cade gave Joker a kick, telling him he could jump off the trail to follow Kit and Navigator. With the Appaloosa's gray fetlocks disappearing ahead of her, Hoku didn't wait for a sign to follow.

Darby hung on around the mustang's neck, burying her face in the filly's mane, feeling it stick to her, gummy with sea spray, as Hoku jumped after Joker.

Before she looked up, Darby heard the snarl of a small engine.

Manny rode a motorcycle out of his taro patch. Yanking the handlebars up, he tried to jump the basin rim and land in their path.

He would have made it if his back tire hadn't hung up on the earthen lip at the same time Manny realized that Kit wasn't about to move.

Manny revved the engine, jerking the back wheel free, but the motorcycle slewed to the left, hurling lumps of mud, then crashed down on its side.

Its engine cut out.

The only sound was wild horses' hooves crossing the wet beach.

Darby couldn't see Kit's face, but she saw Navigator's ears. The brown-black gelding had always reminded her of a knight's charger, and he'd never looked more warlike than he did now.

His rust-edged ears were pinned back in rage. He stamped a forefoot, ridding himself of a blob of red mud that oozed over his shoulder, then trickled down his leg.

Cursing, Manny tried to pull his motorcycle upright, then threw it down in disgust. Shoving his wet hair out of his face, he turned on them, shaking his fists and roaring, "Look what you made me do!"

But then Manny's eyes widened. He took a step backward.

Whatever he'd seen in Kit's face hit him as hard as a fist.

Manny's legs wobbled and, overbalanced by the rifle that was slung on his back, he slipped in the mud. For a second Darby thought he might stay upright, but his feet slid out from under him and Manny splashed down on the seat of his jeans.

Chapter Ten

In the distance, a rooster crowed.

Weird, Darby thought. It wasn't dawn, just the afternoon of a dark and rainy day. The crow must have come from the house that tilted on the hill above the taro patch. She recognized it from the TV news. Cade's mother and stepfather lived there.

Manny stood up. Hurriedly, he fastened the buttons on his thin flannel shirt and wiped at his jeans, making his hands as muddy as his pants.

"Look," he told them, and Darby could tell Manny was going to make excuses before anyone had even said anything to him. "Those nags are eating my only crop. Doin' it at night, and now so pushy they do it in the day. I was only scarin' them off." He waited for a response and when it didn't come, he gestured after the herd and said, "Worked good, yeah?"

Hoku felt so tense beneath Darby, it was as if she rode a horse made of iron.

Navigator's head bobbed up and down as he huffed with wide nostrils. His neck was lathered with nervous sweat. Muscles spasmed in his hindquarters.

Only Joker hung back.

"The stallion and mare are worth something, and they owe me," Manny went on as the rain pattered at his face. "They don't belong to no one, so why not get back some of what I put into this lousy swamp?"

Something's wrong with Navigator, Darby thought. The gelding breathed as if he were moving at a flat-out run.

Kit shifted forward in the saddle and lifted his weight from the gelding's back. He'd noticed trouble, too, Darby thought, but Kit couldn't see the gelding rolling his eyes until they showed white.

"Never occurred to you, I guess, that it might be dangerous," Kit said.

"I'm careful and I'm good," Manny said, jerking his chin up. Then, unwilling to argue with the fore-man, he turned on Cade. "Ask the little paniolo boy. He'll tell you I never liked company."

As if someone had snapped a whip over their rumps, Joker and Hoku startled forward and crowded close to Navigator.

Were all the horses on the island spooked by

Manny? Darby massaged Hoku's withers, then watched Kit for a sign that she should do something else.

But that's not what Darby saw. Sam Forster had told her that the Ely brothers had a reputation for fighting. Now that she was beside Kit, Darby caught his patient, watchful expression. He wasn't being polite; Kit was waiting for Manny to make one wrong move.

A herd of black-and-white-spotted pigs ran squealing in the distance and Manny frowned after them. He kept complaining, saying he might just give up on the place and hoped the state would come red-tag his house and pay him to rip it down.

But his complaints had lost their energy. He looked uneasy.

And then they all felt it.

The earth trembled beneath them. Sheets of stucco crashed off the tan house.

Then it stopped. Darby had never felt a shorter earthquake. But she wasn't relieved.

Menace filled the air. Something bad was coming.

The sound started like a big truck, built to the roar of a train, and a huge and heavy din like a flight of dragons enveloped them.

Manny pointed past the riders. Then he turned and ran.

Navigator hyperventilated and Hoku trembled, but Darby just stared at the beach. It was bare. Only for a second, Darby wondered where the wild horses had gone. Then she saw the wave.

It grew taller by the second, not blue, but brownish green. Dirt and moss from the sea floor lifted in a perfect curl.

It's a tsunami, Darby thought. It came from the east, just as Tutu had said.

Darby stood frozen with fear and awe.

"Go!" Cade's shout and a sound like a hundred million hailstones ended her paralysis.

Just in time, Darby grabbed handfuls of mane along with her rein. Joker galloped past. From the corner of her eye, Darby saw Cade whirling his reins, urging Joker to run flat out.

Hoku saw it, too. Far from shying, she matched Joker's gait. Sorrel and Appaloosa sailed over the taro field's border together. When they landed, Joker dashed ahead. Hoku lowered her forehead against the spray and spatter flying from his heels, and ran after him.

They were headed for the house, or at least the high ground of the hill, Darby thought. Kit and Navigator pounded behind her and Joker was just ahead, sweeping past Manny, but Kit reached a hand down to the man as he neared him.

Kit tried to lift Manny, to save him.

Manny swatted his arm away.

Cade rode low on Joker's neck. "Mom!" he yelled as he reached the house and pulled Joker to a stop.

All three horses crowded together. Hoku bolted up onto the wooden porch, but backed off when a board broke under her hooves. Navigator reared, hitting his head on the awning, and Joker did his best to stay under his rider, though Cade was trying to dismount.

"Let 'em go! Turn 'em loose!" Manny yelled.

Should they? Darby remembered Tutu saying farmers had turned their horses loose a hundred years ago, because there was no time to save them.

Darby looked at Kit.

"Stay aboard if you can," he shouted. "They're safer with us."

Finally, Cade threw himself from Joker's back into the midst of the frightened horses, and tossed his reins to Kit.

The foreman caught them and then Cade was shouldering past the flimsy door.

Breathing just as hard as the horses, Darby looked back at where they'd been.

Where was the wave? It looked more like a flood. Water spilled off the waterfall trail. It rushed in from the ocean and streamed along the road. Water had filled the low taro field so that it looked like a lake. But the gathering wave she'd glimpsed had come ashore elsewhere.

A million questions surged through Darby's mind, but she couldn't gather enough words together to ask even one.

All she understood was Hoku. The filly danced in place, making soft, worried sounds to Navigator.

Now that they'd reached higher ground, the big gelding had quieted. He slung his neck over Hoku's and welcomed Darby's touch on his nose.

"Where is she?" Cade's voice was a growl as he slammed out of the house.

Feeling everyone's eyes on him, Manny glared, then spat.

"Tell me!" Cade reached for Manny and his stepfather tried to block him. Cade winced, but finally gripped the front of his stepfather's sodden shirt.

Darby gasped, but Kit rode closer and added, "Tell him."

"She left."

"Yeah, just like the door hit her and bruised her!" Cade snarled in Manny's face, and he had to lean down to do it.

Was this the first time Cade had realized he had grown taller than the man who'd beaten him?

"Do you see the truck anywhere?" Manny demanded, shoving Cade with both hands. "She stole my truck right after that reporter left."

Cade let go of Manny's shirt and turned back to his horse. He took Joker's reins from Kit and looked over the flooded gulch. A single slab of water lay from here to the ocean.

The water was still rising. Rain pecked at its foamy brown surface, but it climbed the hill by inches instead of feet now. And no water streamed down from behind the house.

If they went that way, Darby thought, they had a chance to escape.

For some reason, Darby recalled this time yesterday in miserable detail. She'd been sinking in gloom over that F on her Creative Writing paper, thinking it was the worst day ever.

The thought made her laugh.

When Cade and Kit looked at her with concern, she shook her head emphatically and said, "Nothing."

Darby didn't know how long they stood there or who noticed the wild horses first. She felt hypnotized. She didn't want to move for fear of disturbing Hoku. And she was so tired, she was pretty sure she'd fall if she tried to dismount.

"Pretty soon *mano*—the shark, yeah?—is going to see he's got a buffet out there," Manny said.

If she'd been holding something, she would have dropped it on Manny's head, Darby thought, but looking down, she saw he had binoculars.

"Can I have a look?" Kit asked.

Darby watched the two men and replayed Kit's words. There'd been no "please," but it had been a request, not a demand. She guessed, under the circumstances, that Kit was calling a truce.

"Not much to see," Manny sneered, as if Kit was wasting his time.

But he handed over the binoculars.

Darby didn't know how long she sat watching the water, lapping like a big tan tongue, just down the hill, but wind off the floodwaters pasted her wet pink shirt against an exposed piece of skin and she shivered.

Looking around, Darby saw she was the only one still on horseback.

Cade caught her attention with a lifted hand, then said, "We put the other horses in the pigpen behind the house. It's in good shape and they don't seem to want to go anywhere."

"Okay," Darby said, but she made no move to dismount.

"How about I walk around and you ride her after me? She's probably too tired out to put up a fuss if I lead her, but—" Cade shrugged.

Head high, sniffing at the unfamiliar posts and plants as they walked, Hoku didn't seem a bit tired. But when the filly didn't object to squeezing past Cade—actually touching him—into the corral with Navigator and Joker, Darby knew the horse wasn't herself.

"We're leaving them saddled and bridled," Cade pointed out. "Just in case we have to ride out in a hurry."

"Why are we staying here?" Darby asked.

Cade took a deep breath and cocked his head sideways.

"Well, we were just talking about that." He said it

as if she should remember, but Darby didn't. "This way," Cade pointed, "is the only way out, and it's a steep, slick climb in the best weather. Which this isn't. Darby?"

"Yeah," she said.

"Just makin' sure you're still with me. You've been sittin' out there lookin' at the water for a long time, and Kit said to leave you be, because you were still shivering."

"What?" Darby asked.

Cade looked relieved at her reaction and went on. "He said that if you had hypothermia, your lips would turn blue and after a while you'd quit shivering. You didn't do either of those, but," he expelled a loud breath and said, "it was weird that the last thing you did before that was laugh."

"I'm okay," Darby assured him. "So, why are we staying here?"

"With the horses tired and dark coming on, this seems like the safest place to be. We'll see what it looks like at dawn and make our plan."

So the gloom surrounding her wasn't storm clouds and rain; it was dusk.

"I don't know about staying here in the dark. What if there's another tidal wave and the water keeps coming up?" Darby asked.

"It won't catch us sleepin'," Cade assured her. "We'll take turns watching. And one thing that rickety house is full of is night spy gear." He sounded disgusted. "Manny's got everything your well-equipped smuggler needs. Spotlights, night-vision goggles, Jet Skis—junk like that. And they all run on batteries. Only thing we're missing is a radio. Since the refrigerator fell on it, I doubt it works too good."

Darby's laugh ended up being a half gulp.

"That was weird, too," she said. "I don't laugh like that."

"It's been a pretty weird day," Cade told her, and his reassuring tone caught Darby's attention. Even though he was hatless and his blond hair had dried in bedraggled strands, he sounded a little more mature. Maybe it was because he'd had a chance to stand up to Manny, but Darby didn't give it too much thought, because her knees locked up when she dismounted.

She had been on Hoku for a long time, she thought, as her boots touched down.

The rain had stopped, and the horses were munching hay that had been spread out on a tarp.

"Here's what you've been waiting for," she told Hoku as the filly shouldered in to eat what the other horses had left.

Joker and Navigator came to Darby with questing noses. "Yeah, I'm fine," she whispered to them. To Cade, she said, "It's a good thing we didn't turn them loose, you know, take Manny's advice."

"You'll find that's usually the case," Cade told her, and this time, Darby found herself laughing outright.

"You sound so sophisticated," she said, and he

joined in the laughter.

It wasn't that funny, but for some reason it took them a long time to stop.

Darby was starting out of the pen, when Hoku nudged her in the back.

"Yes?" Darby asked.

Hoku blew sweet hay breath in her face, then nuzzled her neck. It gave Darby the chills, but in a good way. She imagined Hoku was telling her secrets, reminding her that it wouldn't always be dark and wet, that sometime soon, when the world wasn't covered in water, the two of them would gallop endlessly across this island.

 Chapter Eleven

The wild horses were knee-deep in seawater. They'd gone out to the *kipuka* when the waves receded, but once the tide had come in, it was invisible.

Darby's hands shook as she held the binoculars.

"Get ready for that little one to be missing, come morning," Kit said it gently, and he was probably right.

Each time a wave lapped past the horses on the way to the new shoreline above the taro patch, the foal went under and came up gasping. She could see the inside of its pink mouth.

There were two other foals out there, and they struggled against the waves, too, but her heart ached for this smallest one.

They had to do something, but what?

"Watch my mare," Kit said with admiration.

Darby lifted her eyes from the binoculars, and she wasn't sure what he was talking about until Kit nodded back out to sea.

In the weakening light, Medusa's salt-and-pepper coat looked dark gray.

"She takes lead marin' pretty serious," Cade agreed.

Darby watched as the steeldust mare circled the other horses. She picked her way daintily among them, until there was no room. Then she slid into the water and swam, heavy black mane dragging on the water.

"She's countin' 'em," Kit said. "Eleven all told."

"They can't eat," Darby said, "can they?"

"Or drink," Manny put in. "If it were brackish water it might do, but that's pure salt."

"You don't have to sound so cheerful about it," Darby snapped.

"Who's cheerful?" Manny said, smiling.

Don't waste your energy arguing with him, Darby told herself, but when Manny reached for his binoculars, she pretended not to notice.

The black foal was weaving now. Desperate for sleep, his body moved with the waves. Did his feet even reach the rock?

All at once he was drifting, carried off by the tide. His mother whinnied and launched herself after him.

A huge splash rocked the foal as Black Lava swam past, then curved his massive body around the colt, blocking him. The colt hit his father's shoulder, and then his mother was nudging and pushing him back to the others.

Could they do that once night fell? So many things could go wrong in the darkness. Some horses must have been injured in their headlong run from Crimson Vale. Others would have cut themselves on the knife-sharp lava. If they bled, sharks would come.

Unless—Darby perked up for a minute—the sharks had escaped the tsunami. If the sharks had felt warning vibrations like the other creatures, wouldn't they have fled?

Maybe. But not for long. Horrible Manny was right. Sharks were incredibly efficient predators. Very soon they'd realize the horses were theirs.

Darby handed the binoculars to Cade, then looked back at the hillside behind the house. The structure blocked the view west, but the sun must be setting. It was too dim to do anything but pray that all eleven horses made it through the night.

None of the humans even thought about going inside the house. If the waters rose, they wanted to know at once.

Darby, Kit, and Cade sat close to each other on one end of the porch. The board Hoku had broken lay between them and Manny.

It had been so long since anyone had spoken,

Darby's voice startled them.

"Do you think the tsunami came in at Night Digger Point Beach, like it did before?"

"Before? When?" Manny asked.

"A hundred years ago," Cade said. His tone dared Manny to make fun of her. When his stepfather shook his head, but stayed quiet, Cade answered Darby, "Sure it did, and they knew it was going to. That's why they ran all the way over here."

"Look how much good it did 'em," Manny snorted.

"They're not dead," Cade said.

"Hey! Look there!" Kit pointed at blue lights glimmering far to the east.

Cade bolted to his feet. "It's a helicopter."

"Still got those night-stalker eyes," Manny said with grudging admiration.

"Anybody can see it's a helicopter," Cade said.

That wasn't exactly true, but Darby didn't say so.

"Two of them!" Cade added, and then Darby saw them both.

A beam from one of them swept over the water. She tried to think the silvery light was beautiful, but the water was full of things that shouldn't be there. She didn't try to see what they were.

Manny jumped up and waved his arms.

"What d'you think you're doin'?" Kit said.

"Signaling for rescue," Manny answered. "They're here after us!"

"They might notice if you signaled back with a flashlight," Kit said.

Manny did, and the choppers came closer. One looked highly official, but the other was the blue-and-orange Channel Two news copter. Darby smiled. She'd bet Mark Larson had been at Babe's resort when the tsunami struck and had called in a camera crew. So much for bad publicity, Darby thought, but her smile faded as she thought of the seaside resort and hoped the tsunami hadn't damaged it.

And Aunty Cathy. Why hadn't she thought of her before now? Sure, she'd said the waters couldn't rise as high as 'Iolani Ranch, but she was alone, unless Kimo had decided to stay with her instead of returning home to his father.

Everyone but Darby had kept looking skyward.

"I'm not leaving the horses behind," Cade said flatly.

"'Course not," Kit agreed. "Besides, it's too dangerous for them to land, so they'd have to haul us up on a rope."

"No thanks," Darby said.

"I wouldn't mind being lifted out of here," Manny put in, and Darby noticed that Manny touched a chain around his neck as he did. It was hard for her to believe he wore a religious medal, but his hand cupped it with that kind of reverence.

Neighs echoed all around them as the helicopters hovered.

"They don't like that!" Darby warned.

The cries were coming from the seaward side as well as from Hoku, Navigator, and Joker.

Someone in a dive suit—a rescue swimmer, Darby guessed—crouched in the door of the helicopter, shouting through a bullhorn.

"Do you have any injured?"

"We're fine!" Kit bellowed, then gave a thumbs-up sign and spotlighted it with a flashlight.

The swimmer returned the gesture.

"Okay, we'll get someone out to you at daylight."

It seemed even darker after the helicopters left, and what should have been comforting wasn't. The helicopters couldn't save that little black foal or any of the other horses.

Darby's eyelids popped back open.

"Could the helicopters herd the horses back up here?" she asked.

Manny startled awake at her voice, but Kit didn't sound a bit drowsy as he said, "Maybe, or it could panic 'em. I'm thinking the best thing might be to try to get 'em to follow tame horses, our horses, back in."

"But then, where do they go?" Cade asked. "Crimson Vale's gotta be flooded worse than this."

"Back up to Two Sisters," Darby said, and the idea made her sit up straight against the side of the house. "I saw them up there. They acted totally at home."

"If they can find their way," Cade said, reminding

her of what Tutu had said about landmarks disappearing in mud slides and floods.

It was a dismal and disturbing thing to be thinking about as you fell asleep, Darby thought; really depressing. But she went limp with exhaustion, all the same.

It was the ugliest dawn Darby had ever seen. The taro patch had become a wreckage-filled bay. A fence trailing strands of barbed wire had washed in from somewhere. So had a dead spotted pig, a dead horse, dozens of loose boards, sheets of corrugated aluminum, and rafts of broken branches.

"Our horses are fine," Cade said as Darby started to scramble to her feet. "Already fed. Hoku doesn't seem to have lost her appetite."

"Thanks," Darby said.

"One thing you can always count on a mustang for is eatin'," Kit said. "On the range, they're never sure where that next meal's comin' from."

Despite Kit's good humor, Darby was reluctant to pick up the binoculars and focus on the horses. But she did it, counting the wet and miserable wild horses twice.

"Nine?" She lowered the binoculars as bile rose in her throat.

She couldn't help watching the carcass being pushed forward and drawn back by the tide. It was probably one of Black Lava's herd.

She forced herself to scan the brown lake with her eyes, but she didn't see the black foal anywhere. She tried not to think about what that meant.

Kit had unpacked their saddlebags and spread out the few provisions they'd brought on yesterday's ride. Biting into an apple, Cade glared at his stepfather.

"You're welcome to anything you can find in there." Manny nodded to his house, but no one, not even him, made a move to search the ruined kitchen.

Last night, Darby hadn't been hungry, but now her stomach growled and she grabbed up an apple, too. The last thing she'd eaten had been the granola she'd munched as she'd written her note to Aunty Cathy.

"Oh my gosh!" Darby gasped. "The note I left for Aunty Cathy!"

"What about it?" Cade asked.

"It said—I thought we were riding into Crimson Vale, but then we talked to Tutu and she told us—you don't think they'll be trying to look for us there, do you? That would be way too dangerous!"

"Nothin' to be done about it, if they are," Kit said. "And they won't be lookin' for long. The swimmer said they'd be sendin' someone out to us at daybreak."

"Hope they're drivin' a tank," Manny said.

Darby scanned the area around them, and she had to agree. Getting through the rock piles and mud slides on the dirt road that led from the highway wouldn't be easy.

"How long do you think they can go without water?" Cade asked Kit. They both stood with their thumbs in their pockets, looking out at the wild horses.

"Not long. They're already stressed. You think they'll start drinking the salt water? Darby?"

She was surprised Kit was asking her, but she nodded. If they got thirsty enough, she knew the wild horses would drink whatever they could find.

"They could bring 'em in with boats," Manny said. "They used to do that all the time with cattle."

Boats. What day was it? Sunday? Darby sighed. She wouldn't be going on a boat picnic with the Potter family. She hoped they were all safe.

"Will you look at that?" Kit said.

They all turned at the sound of vehicles convoying through the clearing that had once been a road. A red truck full of firefighters, a white van labeled Department of Agriculture, and a Jeep with no top but a roll bar, which looked like it might have been in a garage fire, appeared at the shoreline that had formed from one edge of the taro patch.

Already on his feet, Kit tucked in his shirt, smoothed a hand over his hair, and replaced his black Stetson at its proper buckaroo angle. Without another word, he began picking his way toward the vehicles.

"I'm going, too!" Darby said, and though she had a faint twinge of misgiving about leaving Cade and his stepfather behind together, she had to follow Kit.

With all these people they could save the remaining wild horses. She just knew it.

Darby had no idea how Kit had made the hike so quickly, but by the time she caught up, one of the firefighters was talking about tsunami damage.

"It's early yet, but it looks like we were lucky this time," he said. "From what we can tell so far, damage is pretty much limited to Crimson Vale and Night Digger Point Beach."

Just like last time, Darby thought.

"We lost some wildlife, but no human lives, as far as we know. You five were the ones we were worried about, and you look safe enough."

"Four," Darby said.

"What?"

"Cade's mom—"

"Dee," Kit put in.

"—left a few days ago, according to Manny," Darby finished.

"We'll have to check that out," the fire chief said.

"Now, we need to help those horses."

Darby turned with a smile to the woman who said this.

Her hair was pulled up in a messy bun, and thick-lensed glasses covered eyes blazing with intelligence.

Kit stepped up beside her. With a joking bow, he

said, "Darby Carter, this is my girl, Cricket Pukai."

"I'm nobody's girl, Ely," the woman said. She ignored the good-natured laughter of those—all men—around her, and shook Darby's hand. "I'm a volunteer with the Hapuna Animal Rescue, and I think I recognize you from the feed store."

"Yeah," Darby said.

"She's more than just a volunteer, she's an expert in animal rescue," Kit said.

"Looks like those horses have done a pretty good job rescuing themselves, yeah?" said one of the firefighters. "Oh, and us?" he said to Darby and Kit. "We're just here for muscle."

The men laughed, but Cricket had picked up on the first part of the firefighter's remark.

"It's not really surprising they saved themselves. Amazing, perhaps, but not surprising.

"After the tsunami in Sri Lanka in 2005, no animal carcasses were found except for those of two working water buffalo. They were harnessed and held back by their owners, but there are eyewitness accounts of elephants screaming and running for higher ground, and most dogs refused to go outdoors in the hour before the tidal wave. Flamingos abandoned their coastal breeding areas, bats and birds darkened the skies, and even zoo animals couldn't be baited out of their shelters."

"Why do they know and we don't?" Darby asked.

"Maybe they have more acute hearing," Cricket

said. "Or maybe we just don't pay attention."

Kit stood a little taller and winked at Darby.

"About that muscle?"

"Right," Cricket said and, after a brief conversation with the Department of Agriculture representative, went on, "We have about two miles of plastic fencing. It's not nearly enough, but it will have to do. We'll unroll it and stake it to portable posts, and do our best to aim the horses toward the Lehua High School football field."

"That's my school," Darby said. Then, when all the adults looked at her, she added, "Not that it matters."

"Mark," Cricket greeted the Channel Two reporter as he pulled up in the news van.

Disheveled, as if he'd been working around the clock in boots and jeans, Mark Larson climbed out and patted Cricket's shoulder. "I'm glad to see you're okay. I heard you were in the thick of things. And Miss Darby Carter. This is a far cry from Sugar Sands Cove Resort, isn't it? Your great-aunt was glad to hear you were safe."

"She was?" Darby asked.

"Last night I spotted you clinging to the porch," the reporter said, gesturing toward the half-ruined house.

Darby, Kit, and the reporter turned as Manny's shout hailed the reporter.

Mark Larson waved a hand in acknowledgment,

but his eyes were on Darby as he asked, "Did you ride your Nevada bronco up here? Babe told me I shouldn't miss a chance to see her."

Darby thought of saying Hoku wasn't at her best right now, but that wasn't true.

"You shouldn't," Darby agreed.

"And you might have a chance to see her in action," Cricket said. "If Darby agrees."

Cricket smiled at her and explained, "We're hoping you, Kit, and—?" She glanced at Kit.

"Cade," he supplied.

"Right," Cricket confirmed. "That you'll ride your domestic horses out to the wild ones."

"My horse loves to swim," Darby said, "but all that, uh, stuff out there . . ."

What would Hoku's wild instincts tell her about water filled with dead things?

"All we can hope is that your horses trust you enough to swim partway out, then turn around and lead the wild ones back in. Then, when you get this far, the plastic fence should act like a chute. We just can't let them return to Crimson Vale yet."

An image of the ancient necklace, swept from the cave and out to sea, crossed Darby's mind. Compared to the horses, she thought, it didn't matter.

"But the stallion and lead mare," Darby said hesitantly, "what if they don't follow us? I don't mean to be bringing up problems," she apologized.

"No, that's good," Cricket said, sounding like she

meant it. "You're thinking like a horse and that helps. If the mare and stallion both hold out, the rest of the herd probably will, too. Then we'll consider mechanical means of herding them," Cricket said. "But not yet. You might tell Mr. Billfish we need to keep all loud, gas-powered vehicles away from them. That usually frightens them more and they stay where they feel safe. For now, they feel safe right out there." She pointed.

"Like horses in a fire?" Darby reasoned.

"Exactly," Cricket said, then her attention shifted to the firefighters as they hammered metal posts into the boggy ground and unrolled plastic fence.

Darby started back to the pigpen, which was their makeshift corral. She wanted to ease Hoku into the idea of more riding under strange circumstances, and she didn't have much time. Though Kit had stayed behind with Cricket, he'd hurry over to join Darby and Cade as soon as it was time to attempt their plan.

Darby played the strategy over and over in her mind, imagining her part in it, hoping Hoku wouldn't pick today to remind Black Lava that she'd attacked him once before.

"Hey, baby," Darby said, smooching to her horse. But Hoku was already leaning against the fence, welcoming her human's familiar shape and smell in these odd surroundings.

All three horses nuzzled Darby as she slipped inside the pen, and it was only because she stood so quietly, letting them take comfort in her presence, that Darby heard Manny and Cade arguing.

"Yeah, kid, because I'm so generous, you can keep your stinkin' reward money and your horse."

"Why is it I don't believe you?"

"Believe what ya want, but you're gonna need it to take care of your mom, 'cause you know she'll come crying to you when I'm gone."

"You're always threatening to leave, but you never follow through," Cade said.

"This time's different," Manny said. "I almost want to tell you."

"I got over wanting to hear your lies a long time ago." Cade's tone was poisonous and Darby swallowed in sympathy, thinking of a little boy who'd craved affection from a jerk like Manny.

She should really let them know she was here, Darby thought. But how? Shout, "Hi, I'm listening"?

Besides, she heard Cade's boots clomp across the damaged porch.

"All you need to know is those quakes shook loose more than my house."

"Okay," Cade said, still walking.

"Some of those old stone altars didn't hold up too good," Manny taunted, "and you know what that means? Exposed treasure, stuff you didn't have to crawl for." Manny gave a hacking laugh. "Still miss those old days. You were such a little sissy—came out of those caves blubbering so hard that you couldn't even talk."

No. How could he have found that ancient necklace? How could he have known it even existed? Darby thought.

Cade knew just how to keep Manny talking. He ignored him.

Manny's pitiful, Darby thought; he just had to keep bragging, hoping some of his words would injure Cade, because he knew he couldn't do it with fists anymore.

"Hey, yeah, and if you believed in this stuff, the circle of life baloney, I bet you'd think all this stuff— earthquakes, volcanoes, and tsunami—is the revenge of the old ones!"

"Well then, you'd better watch out," Cade said.

"Yeah?" Manny asked, and that single word reflected a mood cranked up by Cade's small interest. As soon as she heard it, and the sound of Cade turning to face him, Darby headed for the gate.

"I'm not the one who disturbed 'em in the first place," Manny taunted his stepson. "But I won't turn you in."

"You've never kept your word before. Why would you start now?"

All at once, Darby heard the scuffling of feet.

She stopped, knowing Manny would like nothing better than an audience.

Cloth ripped. She heard a punch connect with skin, then a grunt. She was almost sure Cade had punched his stepfather. When she heard Manny cough and spit, she knew she was right.

But Manny kept taunting Cade. "Haven't you ever heard of honor among thieves?"

"You wouldn't know honor if it came up and bit you," Cade said. He was breathing hard, but it sounded like he was trying to get his temper under control. "Besides, I'm no thief."

"Of course you are. Your respectable friends might not want to hear it, but you are—have been since you were a child."

Cade took a deep breath. "All that means is you were contributing to the delinquency of a minor."

"Me? I'm just selling to the highest bidder, kid, and then, soon as I sell that magic necklace and super power bracelet, I'm outta here."

Bracelet? Darby thought. Was it possible Manny had found a different necklace than the one she'd discovered?

"Those ghosts play hardball, yeah?" Manny asked, contradicting his hint that he didn't believe in the ancestors. "Take a look around and tell me they don't. So, I'm headed for the mainland. Ah-low-ha!" He chuckled.

As she popped around the corner of the tilted house, Darby saw that Cade's hair was loose and his shirt was ripped. Manny's cheekbone was red and already swelling.

"Hi!" Darby pulled her mouth into a smile. "Cade, it's almost time to go, so let me tell you our plan!"

 Chapter Twelve

Low tide came with a price.

The water receded about halfway to its normal shoreline, which meant the horses wouldn't have to swim as far, but the rain came back and brought a cold wind with it.

The wind was so strong, Cade left his prized hala hat behind and Kit, who rarely rode with a stampede strap, fixed one to his black Stetson and knotted it under his chin.

Cade, Kit, and Darby had to do without the waterproof "turnout" coats the firemen had offered. The yellow slickers would flap and scare the horses.

So Darby had goose bumps as they rode three across on the wet sand. She shivered when they came to the water, and Kit went on ahead.

"Adios," he said over his shoulder, and soon Navigator was pushing through the waves, his chest like the prow of a ship.

Cricket had told Kit the horses might follow a single rider, which would put fewer of them in danger if anything should go wrong.

If they didn't follow Navigator, Kit would beckon for Cade to join him.

Darby and Hoku were supposed to stay in shallow water, then turn and gallop toward the plastic fenced chute once the wild horses were moving their way.

Cricket said it was the safest job, but Darby wasn't so sure. Surrounded by her own kind, would Hoku listen to her rider and let the wild ones go ahead?

"You heard him, right?" Cade asked, as soon as Kit was out of earshot, and Darby knew he meant Manny.

Darby hesitated, then said, "Yeah."

"What?" Cade shouted into the wind.

"Yeah!" she repeated, more loudly, and when Cade nodded, she expected him to ask her what she thought they should do. She was ready with an answer. This time, they were telling the police. But Cade asked her something entirely different.

"Why would he tell me that?" Cade asked.

Darby tried to rein Hoku closer to Joker, so that

she didn't have to yell, but the filly squealed and pulled away as if to ask Darby what she'd been thinking.

That's a reminder, Darby scolded herself. *Hoku isn't even a "green-broke" saddle horse. You're riding bareback in a tsunami zone.* She definitely had to ask Jonah how to go about training Hoku to saddle.

But she'd worry about that later. Right now, she had to decide how to answer Cade's question.

"That's easy," Darby called to Cade. "You stood up to him. He's a bully and he can't bear that. All these years—" She wasn't sure how to say what she meant without hurting Cade's feelings or making him mad. Some things weren't meant to be yelled into the wind.

"Anyway, he thought he could get to you that way. He knows you won't leave the horses to go make a police report."

"Think he'll sneak off while we're out here, then?" Cade asked, glancing over his shoulder.

"If we're lucky," she said.

"No way." Cade answered his own question. "Did you see how excited he got when the Channel Two van pulled up and that Mark guy recognized him?"

"He'd better enjoy his fame while he can," Darby shouted. "Don't think I won't get up the nerve to tell Mark Larson the truth."

But Cade stopped listening when Kit's gesture summoned him closer. His heels touched Joker, and the Appaloosa plunged into the waves.

The horses were coming!

This is what it means when your heart's in your throat, she thought. White splashes showed against the gray-brown water as two mares leaped off the rock after Joker.

"Yes!" Darby said, shooting her fist skyward.

In answer to Darby's excitement, Hoku surged into the water.

"Only up to your chest," Darby cautioned the filly. "We can't really swim because we've got to turn around in a minute."

And I'm cold, Darby thought, sucking in a breath. The water wasn't freezing or anything, but the wind on her sea-swept clothes chilled her.

"Careful, girl," Darby said, but Hoku knew enough to avoid debris in the water. Much of it looked like packing material, and Darby hoped birds didn't swoop down and try to eat it.

Darby heard the whining of a motor and looked around. Had Cricket changed her mind and decided to send out a boat? She'd mentioned the possibility of helping struggling colts that way, but Darby had gotten the impression she'd use kayaks or canoes, something quiet.

The news helicopter was back in the air; Mark Larson must be with them. Is that what she'd heard? With the wind's whistling, could she have mistaken it for a—?

Jet Ski.

It was no mistake. Showing off—waving at the helicopter overhead!—Manny came snarling toward them.

It was too much, Darby thought. *Oh, Hoku, I'm sorry.*

The filly's feet touched down. Her head shook from side to side, snatching the halter rope rein from Darby's cold hands. Hoku charged into deeper water, and then she was rearing. Darby made one hopeless grab for her mane, touched it, and slammed down on her back into the water.

The shock of saltwater in her eyes, nose, and mouth was worse than the cold. Worse than that, she collided with the sea floor, then floated.

You're supposed to be a swimmer, she thought. Eyes open and burning, she felt disoriented for a minute.

She wasn't sure which way was up, but then she had it. Hoku over there. Sky—there.

Using all the power in her arms, Darby stroked toward the surface.

It was her hands that saved her from a worse collision with the strip of corrugated iron floating in the water. Her fingertips grazed the debris, telling her to stop or at least slow down, and she tried, but Darby's head still hit the solid object and she reeled clumsily away, blinking and dizzy.

She'd asked too much of Hoku. Too much, but the filly was still there. Did she dare grab on to her?

A wave slapped Darby's face. She didn't go

under, but she choked on the saltwater. It abraded her throat each time she coughed.

She had to cling to something, and there was nothing but Hoku.

Terrified, but unwilling to leave her human, Hoku stared at Darby with white-rimmed eyes.

Darby tried to talk to Hoku, but her mouth kept filling with water and her feet threatened to sink when she lost concentration on kicking. Kicking had always been so automatic, but each splash sounded like chanting, like the ladies draped in black from Darby's nightmares, mourning the loss of the sacred necklace.

Darby's hands arrowed through the water. Only a few feet to go and she could touch Hoku and hold on to her back. If the mustang would tolerate such contact.

There! Her arms were around Hoku's neck and the filly stood still, feet planted on sand that Darby somehow couldn't reach. Blackness closed her field of vision, narrowed it to a keyhole, then a pinpoint. She couldn't see, and she was sinking, swirling into the vortex of a giant's throat. Had she made that up? Mrs. Martindale would never believe . . .

Darby only lost consciousness for a few seconds, and the next thing she saw was Cade, with his blond hair all wet. He was screaming into her face.

She pushed him away.

"I'm fine!"

"Then get on Hoku! The horses are coming!"

The wild horses formed a swimming stampede.

I can do this, Darby thought, pulling herself up on the back of the most magnificent and tolerant filly in the world.

Once she was astride Hoku, Darby listened to another voice.

You'll be okay if you're riding a mustang. Isn't that what Samantha Forster had said?

Something like that, but she really didn't want to be hearing voices after hitting her head, so Darby leaned forward, squeezed her legs around Hoku, and held on tight.

A colossal splash sounded behind them and Darby looked back to see Black Lava heaving through the water. For a second, the stallion's eyes— one blue and one brown—stared at Hoku, but this time even Darby knew there was no flirtation in them.

Get out of the way or get in line behind me. The stallion's meaning was as clear as if he'd spoken, and this time Hoku moved aside, too tired to fight. She let her feet touch down and the stallion swam on, creating a swell as high as the waves.

Darby counted the horses following him. A bay and chestnut came first, tails floating. Next, black and dun, shoulders slapped wetly together, but that was all. Wait. Black Lava and four mares? There had been nine horses this morning.

She looked back and saw two mares with foals, struggling, nosing their babies as Cade and Kit swam their mounts alongside. Each time the cowboys urged their geldings closer, the mares rose, wide-mouthed from the water, protecting their babies.

And then Darby saw human arms come out of the water and clasp one of the foals. It took a minute to make sense of it.

The arms belonged to Duckie, Darby's cousin Duxelles Borden, and she was gently side-stroking to a boat. The boat carried Ann and her parents.

Feeling woozy and unsure of herself, Darby looked after Black Lava and the mares before she returned Ann's wave.

Was she really seeing what she thought she was?

Duckie slipped over the side of the boat, going back for the last foal with a smug grin. Yes, that expression proved it was Duckie.

Then Ann shouted, "I suppose you forgot the chocolate-chip cookies!"

Teeth chattering, Darby called back, "Oh, rats!"

"Rats?" Ann giggled and Darby thought they both might be a little hysterical, but the good news was, this was no hallucination. Ann and her family had rowed close enough to help. And all the horses were accounted for, including a third foal, which lay in Mrs. Potter's arms, taking a bottle.

He was ink black and tiny, the smallest of Black Lava's sons.

"You found him!" Darby said.

"All alone, on Night Digger Point Beach! Curled up in the sand, practically camouflaged!" Ann called.

"I'm so glad!" Darby said, and there was so much sea spray on her face, even she didn't know if she was crying.

Only Medusa stayed behind, alone on the lava spit.

"It's the helicopters and the Jet Ski and all the noise!" Kit said once they'd slogged ashore.

A conservancy volunteer radioed Cricket that all of the horses thus far had arrived at Lehua High School and were voraciously eating the turf of the football field.

With three foals unloaded from the Potters' boat into their horse trailer and on their way to join the rest of the herd, only Medusa was missing.

"We've done really well," Cricket said.

"I'm not leaving her behind," Kit insisted. "That steeldust has the heart of a lion."

Darby sat in the filthy sand, holding Hoku's rein and looking up at Kit and Cricket.

Cricket looked speechless, but she got over it in a hurry.

"Of course we won't leave her, but . . ." Cricket frowned. She paced. She took down her bun and wound it back up even more messily.

"I know what to do, but I don't know how," she mumbled.

"Tell me," Kit said.

"Put cotton in her ears. It's the only thing we haven't tried. She's terrified of the helicopters, and now that her herd's out of sight, she'll probably just hunker down and stay where she is. If it isn't impossible—but it is."

"No, ma'am, it's not." Kit drew a breath as if he were about to begin a long story. "My major talent in life is bronc ridin', and those skills are pretty much good for nothin'—except this." Kit stared out to the spit. The mare neighed frantically for her herd. "I betcha I could get cotton in her ears, if I had any."

Cricket was already rummaging in the back of the ugly Jeep. She pulled out a medical kit and a pouf of cotton nearly as big as her head.

"Will that do?" she asked.

"We'll see," he said. Kit sat down on the sand and shucked off his boots and socks.

"You can't walk on lava rock barefooted," Cricket told him.

"Well, I can't swim in my boots," Kit said. He took the waterproof pack Cricket handed him and shrugged it on. Then he turned to Navigator. "Once more, boy? It's the thanks we get for being so big and strong."

Navigator stood still, regarding Kit as if they were equals.

"Okay," Kit said. Then, as if Navigator had told him to, he made a few quick jerks on saddle leather and passed his heavy Western saddle to a firefighter. "Mind watching that?"

"No problem," the guy said with a smile.

Reaching high for a handful of the gelding's black mane, Kit pushed off his bare feet and, with a light and graceful jump that reminded Darby that the foreman had Shoshone ancestors, Kit leaped aboard the big bay.

"Wow," Darby said, and she heard Cade and Cricket make sounds of admiration, too.

Astride Navigator's broad back, Kit leaned forward, unbuckled the gelding's headstall and lowered it until the bit cleared the gelding's mouth. That, he handed to Cade.

"Now you're just showing off," Cricket said. Kit rode the gelding out just as he had before. The only difference was that he guided Navigator with hands and legs instead of metal and leather.

The sun peeked through the clouds for a moment. As clearly as a mirror, the wet beach reflected horse and rider until they reached the water and Navigator began to swim.

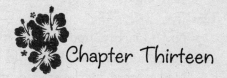 Chapter Thirteen

Kit swam the gelding within about a hundred yards
of Medusa before he slid off into the water.

"He just patted the bay on the rump, and now he's
swimming to the mare," Cricket reported as she
looked through binoculars.

"Wouldn't swim in that junk soup if you paid me,"
said one of the firefighters. Shaking his head, he lowered his own binoculars, and he must have noticed
Darby squinting and shading her eyes, trying to
watch, because he handed them to her.

"Oh, wow, thanks!" Darby said.

As she watched, Kit glared at the helicopter overhead. Medusa's head fell lower, as if she could escape
the huge, noisy insect.

Darby focused on Kit as he tugged down his wet shirtsleeves, covered his hands with them as well as he could, then pulled himself up on the rock. He seemed to be talking to himself as he walked, tender-footed, toward the gray horse.

"You can't read lips, can you?" Cricket asked Darby.

"No!" Darby almost dropped her binoculars as she looked at Cricket. "What did he say?"

"Never mind," Cricket said without lowering her binoculars, but she was smiling until she muttered, "They're circling each other."

There still must have been some vegetation from the spit's life as a *kipuka*, Darby thought, because Kit appeared to be fighting for balance as he shed the waterproof backpack.

Medusa backed away from the man, but as soon as her hooves struck water, she bolted forward.

Kit had cotton balled up in each hand now. Medusa's ears were flattened and her teeth were bared. Horse and man watched for a chance to charge.

"Please, let me look," Cade said, jiggling Darby's shoulder.

Darby tightened her hold on the borrowed binoculars and said, "You have great eyes."

"Nobody—" Cade began, but just then Cricket yelped.

Darby couldn't help looking at her.

"I don't think he can— Oh!" Cricket leaned forward as if she could get her eyes even closer to her lenses, and her hands covered her mouth.

"Thanks," Cade said, lifting the binoculars' strap off over Darby's head.

"I can't fight you for them," Darby protested, trying to sound pitiful.

"Good," Cade said.

Darby wanted to smack him, but that wouldn't be productive. Besides, she was trying to remember where Kit had put Manny's binoculars. She was pretty sure he'd had them last.

She hurried around, looking everywhere for the binoculars and because she was the only one who wasn't watching Kit and Medusa, she was the only one who saw Manny haul his Jet Ski out of the water. Then, he fumbled at that medal or whatever it was that hung on a chain around his neck.

Relieved the racket had stopped, she was about to ask Manny if he knew where his binoculars were. But she knew he'd keep them away from her out of spite.

Hands on her hips, Darby looked around. Another few minutes and all the excitement would be over! This was like a bad dream. Why couldn't she— There!

Darby spotted the binoculars dangling from a fire engine's outside mirror, and ran to snag them. She tried holding them up to her eyes as she ran closer, to the edge of the water, but she tripped and fell to one knee.

Rubbing the bridge of her nose, which she'd hit with the binoculars, she got up slowly.

Kit was already on Medusa! He must have just landed on her back, because the steeldust mare's head shot up in outrage. With his legs clamped around her, Kit made one lightning-fast move. Both arms snapped forward, stuffed cotton in her ears, and then he clung to her mane with one hand, ready for her to buck.

Instead, Medusa stood, puzzled and still.

The wild mare was thinking, Darby decided, trying to make sense of all this madness.

Just then, Navigator swam toward her rock. The gelding must have waited for Kit, even though the foreman had urged him to swim off. Now his front hooves scrambled at the lava rock.

Poor tired horse. He was trying to pull himself up on firm footing, Darby thought.

Medusa might have no idea why her world had crashed out of control, but she knew how to treat an intruder.

She lunged at Navigator. The gelding fell back, but never submerged before veering away. He gave up on Kit and swam for shore.

Medusa wasn't done with him. Eyes rolling white with anger, as if Navigator's trespass was the final insult, Medusa launched herself into the sea.

White foam bloomed all around her as she chased the Quarter Horse.

Medusa hated having Kit on her back, but she was fighting two enemies. Neck outstretched, gray chin grazing the waves, she tried to catch up with the much bigger gelding.

She raised her chin and pulled her chest partway from the water as she threw her heavy head back, trying to strike Kit's forehead. The mare made a last try for Navigator, then swam in a circle, mouth agape, reaching for Kit's leg.

Kit managed to stay out of reach, but barely.

At last, Navigator gained the shore and Darby realized she'd stopped using the binoculars. As soon as Medusa emerged from the water it was clear why she'd been slower and why she didn't buck.

Blood streamed from her legs. Because she couldn't run after her herd, she called to them. Her legs were unsteady even after Kit dismounted, but it was her heartbroken whinny that made Darby lean closer to Hoku.

"I hurt her bad," Kit told Cricket.

To Darby, it sounded like the foreman might cry, but Cricket's answer was brisk.

"Not so bad," Cricket said. "Nothing that a few snips and sutures won't mend. And it wasn't your fault, anyway. It was that lava rock."

"I want to adopt her," Kit said, looking at the suffering horse. "Does the conservancy allow that?"

"You've earned her, it seems to me," Cricket said simply.

Kit stood openmouthed for a few seconds, and then he and Cade settled down to hold the mare while Cricket sedated her.

As they waited for the drug to work, Cricket glanced up at Darby.

"I almost forgot, I was radioed that Jonah's back on the island—who knows how he managed that! I'd heard all air traffic was being held on Oahu—and he and—some others—are coming over here. Something like that. Sorry, I'm not much of a secretary."

"It's okay," Darby said, and then for some reason she yawned. "I'm gonna put the horses back in that pen."

Cade and Kit nodded.

As Darby rode Hoku, Joker and Navigator followed her toward the pen.

"You're ponying, sort of," she praised Hoku as they approached the leaning house.

The gate to the pen was open and Navigator and Joker plodded inside, intent on finding food, but they both shied as Manny emerged from the pen, pursuing some small animal.

As soon as she saw Manny, an archaic expression of Darby's dad's popped into her mind.

I have a bone to pick with you, he'd say when he'd been saving up errors for way too long. And that's just how Darby felt. Hoku had been frightened by his

Jet Ski and she'd bucked Darby into the chaotic sea. She and her horse could both have been injured.

Before she told him off, though, Darby tried to see what Manny was after.

It was black and white and about the size of a hot dog bun, Darby thought. Its ear-piercing squeal told her Manny had succeeded in kicking it. And it was a piglet.

Darby thought she might scream, too. By its coloring and location, the piglet was an orphan. She'd seen a black-and-white sow washed up this morning, and this baby was alone.

"Stop!" Darby yelled when Manny pulled his foot back to kick the piglet again. "You can't do that."

"Who says?"

"I do," Darby told him.

"Tough luck, kid, it's my pig. Besides, I wouldn't have to kick it if it'd stay out of my way."

It's probably hungry, Darby thought, *and it's looking for its mother.* But she didn't say that because her mind was filled with what she knew.

"Do you know what they call that? The way you're talking? 'An abuser mentality,'" Darby told him. "You can't take responsibility for your own actions, so you—"

"Shut up!" he snapped.

She didn't expect his arm to shoot out toward Hoku, but it did, and there was no way she'd let him touch her horse!

Hoku shied. Darby lunged to knock Manny's hand away, but she leaned out too far and accidentally slid off Hoku's back. As she slipped, she managed to knock Manny down.

Hoku trotted the few yards to the other horses and stopped just inside the pigpen. Darby made it to her feet before Manny did. She stumbled after her horse, shut the gate, and locked it.

Then, with Hoku safe, Darby rushed toward the miserable piglet and, in a single swoop, caught it and held it against her chest. It was warm and wiggly, but quiet.

"Put that pig down," Manny snapped. His palms and heels slipped in the mud as he struggled to get up. "It's mine."

"Not anymore," Darby said, and then she ran.

Call it the coward's way out, Darby thought, but she wasn't going to let Manny hurt anything else small and helpless, and she couldn't stop him on her own. She raced back toward the Department of Agriculture van and the fire engine. She was looking for help, when she rammed into Jonah.

"Oh, I'm so glad to see you!" Darby gasped.

"That's because you weren't with him in the airport, when my trip and all of the flights home were canceled simultaneously," Megan interrupted.

"I'm glad to see you too, sis," Darby said, but Jonah was watching her with something between relief and suspicion, so she kept her eyes on him, not Megan.

"We got here just in time to see you fall on Manny. Nice work," Megan said, holding her hand out for Darby to slap it in solidarity. But she couldn't. She was holding Pigolo.

Oh, man, if she'd named it, the piglet had to be hers.

"I didn't fall," Darby corrected her. "I tackled him."

"No," Jonah said, edging into the conversation. "We saw Hoku spook, then saw you—"

"Tackle him," Darby said, and Pigolo added his voice to her side.

"Oh my gosh, is that a pig?" Megan demanded.

"A piglet," Darby corrected as her eyes darted toward Jonah. "And his name is Pigolo."

Manny held the arm of a uniformed Department of Agriculture officer, half dragging him toward Darby.

"She stole my pig. Can't you arrest her or something?"

"Did you steal his pig?" the officer asked, and Manny finally relinquished his grip on the man's arm.

Darby looked down at the sweet spotted back. Pink skin showed between the black blotches, and white hair glazed over it. Poor little thing.

"I did," she admitted. "He was kicking it."

"It's my pig," Manny insisted.

"Just like that black stud and the steeldust mare are your horses?" the officer asked.

Manny looked trapped. He wasn't sure what to say.

"Yeah?" he guessed, finally.

"Super-duper," the man said, and now he grabbed Manny's wrist. "If you'll just step over here, Mr. Billfish, we need to have a talk about why you didn't remove your horses from this area when you were under an evacuation order."

"Because they weren't—" Manny's protests grew quieter as he was led away.

"Pigolo." Jonah folded his arms and looked at the little animal burrowed closer to Darby.

"Yes." Darby didn't know what else to say.

Jonah's eyebrows came down, making a threatening black line across his forehead.

"I was just thinking that's what we needed. A wild pig. We don't have enough of 'em tearin' things up and goin' rabid on us."

"I'll watch him," Darby promised.

"No, I mean it. Good work, Granddaughter. Just for that, you and Pigolo sit here and relax. Me 'n' Megan will go get the horses."

Megan rolled her eyes and followed Jonah, shaking her head as he kept on talking.

"At least Francie the useless goat will be glad to see him, and I won't have to hear any more about barbecuing her for Fourth of July dinner . . ."

Darby lowered her lips to kiss the piglet's head and whispered, "We're not eating you. I promise."

Chapter Fourteen

All at once, vehicles moved all around Darby.

Jonah backed up a truck and trailer to load Hoku and Joker. Another news van arrived, while the Channel Two helicopter whipped the trees into a frenzy, and gravel rose in a wet sandstorm, pelting animals and people alike before it set down.

Darby held her hair out of her eyes, trying to keep the last few strands in her ponytail.

When the rotors on the helicopter wound down, Mark Larson jumped out and said, "Let's go! Go!" Darby gasped. It looked as if the blade-edged rotors came within inches of Mark's head.

When the helicopter's rotors came to a stop and

its engine was turned off, the silence felt like pressure in Darby's ears.

"Set up there, yeah, perfect!" the reporter said, then cautioned, glancing up the beach at a grape-colored van, "Not too close. Don't scare the horse, yeah? She's in a bad way."

The reporter positioned himself with Cade, Kit, and Cricket working on Medusa in the background, then nodded at his cameraman.

"The rescue of the mustangs of Wild Horse Island has caught the imagination of the world," Mark said. "First, viewers saw the havoc a five-point-two magnitude earthquake can bring to a four-star resort like Sugar Sands Cove. Next, from the skies over Crimson Vale and Crescent Cove, they saw the aftermath of a tragic tsunami and the stranding of horses and humans alike, by dangerous storm waters.

"Now Channel Two is proud to bring you the heart-stopping rescue, after forty-eight tense hours, of Hawaii's last wild horses."

Mark Larson fell silent, watching over his camera-man's shoulder, and Darby guessed that people in front of their TVs were seeing a replay of earlier footage, just as she was.

Darby watched the horses' rescue as it happened. Hoku looked bright and beautiful, and if she hadn't recognized her horse, she wouldn't have believed that was her riding. She looked adventurous and strangely at home on the beautiful filly.

Minutes later, though, as the horses began swimming toward safety, Darby was still watching Hoku when she saw Manny showing off and waving from his Jet Ski.

And then the reporter was narrating again, "Here we see Mr. Manuel Billfish—regular viewers will recall from an earlier Channel Two interview that his family's house was all but destroyed by earlier earthquakes, and wild horses had trampled his taro fields.

"And yet he attempts to rescue a wild horse which a young woman volunteer has been unable to control."

"No, he did not," Darby said.

"*Shh!*" someone hissed.

Pigolo had been sleeping, but now his sharp little hooves peddled against Darby's shirt and she held him away from her body. He gave a high-pitched grunt as if he was about to break into a squeal, but when someone shushed her again, Darby had to speak up. "That waving—he wasn't herding the horse. He was just showing off for your camera."

Darby's mind spun faster than her mouth. She wanted to explain how Manny had spooked Hoku— her horse and not a wild Hawaiian horse—causing her to fall, but all Darby could do was sputter, "R-rescue?"

Mark pointed to the cameraman.

Darby didn't know what the gesture signified, but the reporter leaned close to her and said, "Honey, I promise to talk with you. Even do corrections if they're warranted, but my editor will have my head if I don't get these up-to-the minute shots out before *they* do. That other news team flew in from Oahu."

He jabbed an index finger toward the purple van Darby had spotted before. Maybe because he was younger than she'd thought, Darby felt a little sympathetic.

"And it would be nice," he added, "if they could hear me instead of your little friend."

"Okay," Darby said. Just then, Megan walked up and Darby handed Pigolo off to her. Darby whispered, "Do you know where he is right now? They just took him to jail!"

The news reporter looked shocked for only a few seconds. Then his lips pressed together hard. "Stick around, yeah?"

"Don't worry," Darby said, but then Mark continued the story as if they'd never talked to each other.

"Here we see, while Mr. Billfish attempts to save the horse, a blond woman rescues the unlucky girl—"

Blond woman? That was Cade!

Unlucky girl? That was her!

Cade pulled his hala hat down past his eyebrows and stormed off toward Jonah's truck.

Megan bumped her shoulder against Darby's, then jerked her head to a place farther off, where they could talk.

"I've seen enough, anyway," Darby said. She took the piglet back as she followed her friend.

She sure didn't expect Megan's first words.

"Should I be jealous?" Megan asked.

"Of Pigolo?" Darby said. "Are you nuts?"

Megan shook her head. "This isn't funny to me."

"I'm not trying to be funny."

"I'm talking about that," Megan said, pointing back to the cameraman.

Darby thought really hard. What had she missed?

"Cade," Megan said finally. Darby pictured Cade, with his loose hair and shirt half gone, pulling her head above the water. To Megan, it might have looked like a romantic rescue.

"I don't like Cade," Darby said, trying to keep her voice from going about ten octaves higher in surprise. "Not like that! Do you know what he was saying to me? Something like, 'If you're not dead, get on your horse and get out of the way.'"

"He did not," Megan said, half laughing.

"That's what it sounded like," Darby said seriously.

"So you don't *like* like him?"

"That's what I said!" Darby insisted.

"And you'd rather kiss Pigolo than Cade?" Megan asked.

Darby stared at her friend and decided this might be the best example in the world that jealousy could make people crazy. Then she planted a big noisy kiss on Pigolo's black-and-white head.

"Okay," Megan said, shifting from foot to foot. "I'm going to see if I can cheer him up."

Darby was still staring after Megan and trying to ignore Jonah's beckon to hurry up and join them when Mark approached her.

Loosening his tie and looking kind of grim, he said, "Spill it, yeah? I want to hear what you have to say, because this story is going national in a day or two, and it has got to be perfect."

It turned out that the story actually aired nationally a week later, but that wasn't the most important thing to happen that day.

Early on that morning, Darby, Cade, Megan, and Jonah rode with Tutu and Uncle Kindy to Crimson Vale.

The flooded road had finally opened, and though the wild horses hadn't returned, the oldest members of the group had decreed this to be the best day to enter the valley in search of the ancient necklace.

Uncle Kindy, a small, pear-shaped man whose sense of humor contrasted with his somberness over things spiritual, had determined that he and Tutu must enter the cave behind Shining Stallion Falls alone.

Whether or not the ancient necklace still lay where Darby had left it, the cave had to be purified.

"No offense," he'd told Darby, "but you should

not have entered. That was wrong."

If they found the necklace, it would be moved to a higher, more secure place.

Cade, Jonah, Megan, and Darby listened as the two old voices echoed off the cave walls. The ancient language twined in two tones, sounding eerie but comforting. The ceremony evoked every emotion a human could feel.

They didn't see Tutu and Uncle Kindy leave the cave or begin climbing with their walking sticks, but they'd been waiting for the old pair for nearly two hours when Navigator, Kona, and Tango began to neigh.

All the horses were staring at a spot high and to the left of the waterfall. "What do they see?" Megan asked Jonah,

Jonah shook his head. Then Tutu appeared coming down a trail, with her pink shawl billowing around her. Uncle Kindy descended on another trail, but when the two elders reached level ground again, they declared, "It is done."

Darby couldn't ask if they meant there'd be no more earthquakes, tsunamis, or other disasters. She knew that couldn't happen, but she breathed more easily and she felt more settled. Something out of balance had been set right.

Cade refused to come in and watch the TV special about Wild Horse Island's tsunami. Only five minutes would be devoted to the wild horse rescue, but he claimed a headstall needed repair and polish, and nothing would persuade him to come inside Sun House.

The rest of the family took their dinner plates into the living room. They watched as the story of the tsunami was told from every possible angle — scientific to supernatural.

At last, they saw a repetition of the story Mark Larson had shown live on the day Medusa was brought in.

"She looked bad," Kit said at the sight of the willful mare being stitched up on the shore.

"You're making progress," Jonah said, and though he didn't watch his foreman's face light up, Darby did.

The report ended with Mark Larson strolling along a windy beach still littered with debris.

"Many stories emerged within the larger story," Mark said. He told some of them, then thanked the members of the Kealoha family of 'Iolani Ranch, Cricket Pukai, the Potter family, and Duxelles Borden.

"And I inadvertently made a local man a hero," Mark Larson said. "I regret that Manuel Sharp — Billfish was only one of his aliases — hoodwinked this reporter, but now I'll reveal the truth.

"Mr. Sharp is under arrest for several charges, including felony possession of antiquities, numerous firearm violations, and domestic abuse. It's impossible to say which of these charges is worst, but this reporter finds it pleasingly ironic that Sharp's ticket for not removing his animals from a danger zone was responsible for authorities finding the pouch around his neck, which contained two ancient, sacred artifacts he had already offered for sale on the Internet.

"Among the many unsung heroes of the day, this reporter would like to spotlight Darby Kealoha Carter. According to a friend known only as 'pig girl,' the teenager is called 'can-do *keiki*' by some local paniolos.

"When asked if she wasn't scared during the water rescue aboard an unproven young horse, Miss Carter, a student at Lehua High School, said, 'Sure, of sharks, but it would have been wrong to leave the horses out there.'"

In the last shot, the camera showed Mark's feet stepping over vines which had already reclaimed the beach.

"Coming to you live from the newly opened road into Crimson Vale, this is Mark Larson."

"He's nice," Aunty Cathy said as the credits rolled on the TV screen over a series of still photographs. "But way too dramatic."

"And who's this pig girl?" Jonah asked. "I would have guessed Darby."

"Who knows," Megan said, shrugging. "But it's weird she knew about Darby's nickname, because—"

She broke off and they all saw a photograph of Megan, unmistakable because of her cherry Coke–colored hair, and the black-and-white piglet in her arms.

"Pig girl? In my interview I say that nice can-do *keiki* stuff," Megan shrieked, turning on Darby, "and you say I go by pig girl?"

"Megan!" Aunty Cathy said.

"What, Mom? Thanks to her, I can never go to school again."

"Not me!" Darby said, jumping to her feet.

"Who else would call me that?" Megan demanded.

"Girls!" Aunty Cathy cautioned as Megan chased Darby from the room.

When Darby realized Megan was laughing, she let herself be tackled. Then Megan fell down, too, and they laughed and held their sides until Darby agreed to do all Megan's nighttime chores for her, even though Mark Larson had clearly gotten the error someplace else.

Doing chores by moonlight wasn't so bad, Darby decided later.

In fact, seeing her horse outlined with silvery light was magical.

"That mare of yours," Jonah said from out of the darkness. "She's got a good head on her, but she needs to grow up, yeah?"

With a throaty neigh, Hoku reared.

"I guess," Darby said, knowing Jonah might take her words as agreement.

With Hoku's spirit crackling all around her, Darby saw the stars as silver sparks and she knew she didn't want her horse to grow up one minute faster.

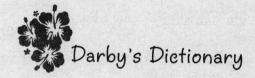

Darby's Dictionary

In case anybody reads this besides me, which it's too late to tell you not to do if you've gotten this far, I know this isn't a real dictionary. For one thing, it's not all correct, because I'm just adding things as I hear them. Besides, this dictionary is just to help me remember. Even though I'm pretty self-conscious about pronouncing Hawaiian words, it seems to me if I live here (and since I'm part Hawaiian), I should at least try to say things right.

<u>ali'i</u> — AH LEE EE — royalty, but it includes chiefs besides queens and kings and people like that

'aumakua — OW MA KOO AH — these are family guardians from ancient times. I think ancestors are supposed to come back and look out for their family members. Our 'aumakua are owls and Megan's is a sea turtle.

chicken skin — goose bumps

da kine — DAH KYNE — "that sort of thing" or "stuff like that"

hanai — HĀNYE E — a foster or adopted child, like Cade is Jonah's, but I don't know if it's permanent

haole — HOW LEE — a foreigner, especially a white person. I get called that, or *hapa* (half) *haole*, even though I'm part Hawaiian.

hapa — HA PAW — half

hewa-hewa — HEE VAH HEE VAH — crazy

hiapo — HIGH AH PO — a firstborn child, like me, and it's apparently tradition for grandparents, if they feel like it, to just take *hiapo* to raise!

hoku — HO COO — star

holoholo — HOE LOW HOW LOW — a pleasure trip that could be a walk, a ride, a sail, etc.

honu — HO NEW — sea turtle

'iolani — EE OH LAWN EE — this is a hawk that brings messages from the gods, but Jonah has it painted on his trucks as an owl bursting through the clouds

ipo — EE POE — sweetheart, actually short for *ku'uipo*

kanaka — KAH NAW KAH — man

kapu — KAH POO — forbidden, a taboo

keiki — KAY KEY — really, when I first heard this, I thought it sounded like a little cake! I usually hear it meaning a kid, or a child, but Megan says it can mean a calf or colt or almost any kind of young thing.

lanai — LAH NA E — this is like a balcony or veranda. Sun House's is more like a long balcony with a view of the pastures.

lau hala — LA OO HA LA — some kind of leaf in shades of brown, used to make paniolo hats like

Cade's. I guess they're really expensive.

lei — LAY E — necklace of flowers. I thought they were pronounced LAY, but Hawaiians add another sound. I also thought leis were sappy touristy things, but getting one is a real honor, from the right people.

lei niho palaoa — LAY NEEHO PAH LAHOAH — necklace made for old-time Hawaiian royalty from braids of their own hair. It's totally *kapu*—forbidden—for anyone else to wear it.

luna — LOU NUH — a boss or top guy, like Jonah's stallion

mahalo — MAW HA LOW — thank you

menehune — MEN AY WHO NAY — little people

ohia — OH HE UH — a tree like the one next to Hoku's corral

pali — PAW LEE — cliffs

paniolo — PAW NEE OH LOW — cowboy or cowgirl

pau — POW — finished, like Kimo is always asking,

"You *pau*?" to see if I'm done working with Hoku or shoveling up after the horses

Pele — PAY LAY — the volcano goddess. Red is her color. She's destructive with fire, but creative because she molds lava into new land. She's easily offended if you mess with things sacred to her, like the ohia tree, lehua flowers, 'ohelo berries, and the wild horse herd on Two Sisters.

pueo — POO AY OH — an owl, our family guardian. The very coolest thing is that one lives in the tree next to Hoku's corral.

pupule — POO POO LAY — crazy

tutu — TOO TOO — great-grandmother

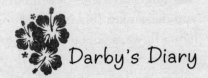
Darby's Diary

<u>Ellen Kealoha Carter</u>—my mom, and since she's responsible for me being in Hawaii, I'm putting her first. Also, I miss her. My mom is a beautiful and talented actress, but she hasn't had her big break yet. Her job in Tahiti might be it, which is sort of ironic because she's playing a Hawaiian for the first time and she swore she'd never return to Hawaii. And here I am. I get the feeling she had huge fights with her dad, Jonah, but she doesn't hate Hawaii.

<u>Cade</u>—fifteen or so, he's Jonah's adopted son. Jonah's been teaching him all about being a paniolo. I thought he was Hawaiian, but when he took off his hat he had blond hair—in a braid! Like old-time

vaqueros—weird! He doesn't go to school, just takes his classes by correspondence through the mail. He wears this poncho that's almost black it's such a dark green, and he blends in with the forest. Kind of creepy the way he just appears out there. Not counting Kit, Cade might be the best rider on the ranch.

Hoku kicked him in the chest. I wish she hadn't. He told me that his stepfather beat him all the time.

<u>Cathy Kato</u>—forty or so? She's the ranch manager and, really, the only one who seems to manage Jonah. She's Megan's mom and the widow of a paniolo, Ben. She has messy blond-brown hair to her chin, and she's a good cook, but she doesn't think so. It's like she's just pulling herself back together after Ben's death.

I get the feeling she used to do something with advertising or public relations on the mainland.

<u>Jonah Kaniela Kealoha</u>—my grandfather could fill this whole notebook. Basically, though, he's harsh/nice, serious/funny, full of legends and stories about magic, but real down-to-earth. He's amazing with horses, which is why they call him the Horse Charmer. He's not that tall, maybe 5'8", with black hair that's getting gray, and one of his fingers is still kinked where it was broken by a teacher because he spoke Hawaiian in class! I don't like his "don't touch the horses unless they're working for you" theory, but it totally works. I need to figure out why.

<u>Kimo</u>—he's so nice! I guess he's about twenty-five, Hawaiian, and he's just this sturdy, square, friendly guy. He drives in every morning from his house over by Crimson Vale, and even though he's late a lot, I've never seen anyone work so hard.

<u>Kit Ely</u>—the ranch foreman, the boss, next to Jonah. He's Sam's friend Jake's brother and a real buckaroo. He's about 5'10" with black hair. He's half Shoshone, but he could be mistaken for Hawaiian, if he wasn't always promising to whip up a batch of Nevada chili and stuff like that. And he wears a totally un-Hawaiian leather string with brown-streaked turquoise stones around his neck. He got to be foreman through his rodeo friend Pani (Ben's buddy). Kit's left wrist got pulverized in a rodeo fall. He's still amazing with horses, though.

<u>Megan Kato</u>—Cathy's fifteen-year-old daughter, a super athlete with long reddish-black hair. She's beautiful and popular and I doubt she'd be my friend if we just met at school. Maybe, though, because she's nice at heart. She half makes fun of Hawaiian legends, then turns around and acts really serious about them. Her Hawaiian name is Mekana.

<u>The Zinks</u>—they live on the land next to Jonah. They have barbed-wire fences and their name doesn't sound Hawaiian, but that's all I know.

<u>Tutu</u>—my great-grandmother. She lives out in the rain forest like a medicine woman or something, and she looks like my mom will when she's old. She has a pet owl.

<u>Aunt Babe Borden</u>—Jonah's sister, so she's really my great-aunt. She owns half of the family land, which is divided by a border that runs between the Two Sisters. Aunt Babe and Jonah don't get along, and though she's fashionable and caters to rich people at her resort, she and her brother are identically stubborn. Aunt Babe pretends to be all business, but she loves her cremello horses and I think she likes having me and Hoku around.

<u>Duxelles Borden</u>—if you lined up all the people on Hawaii and asked me to pick out one NOT related to me, it would be Duxelles, but it turns out she's my cousin. Tall (I come up to her shoulders), strong, and with this metallic blond hair, she's popular despite being a bully. She lives with Aunt Babe while her mom travels with her dad, who's a world-class kayaker. About the only thing Duxelles and I have in common is we're both swimmers. Oh, and I gave her a nickname—Duckie.

❧ ANIMALS! ❧

<u>Hoku</u>—my wonderful sorrel filly! She's about two and a half years old, a full sister to the Phantom, and boy, does she show it! She's fierce (hates men) but smart, and a one-girl (ME!) horse for sure. She is definitely a herd-girl, and when it comes to choosing between me and other horses, it's a real toss-up. Not that I blame her. She's run free for a long time, and I don't want to take away what makes her special.

She loves hay, but she's really HEAD-SHY due to Shan Stonerow's early "training," which, according to Sam, was beating her.

Hoku means "star." Her dam is Princess Kitty, but her sire is a mustang named Smoke and he's mustang all the way back to a "white renegade with murder in his eye" (Mrs. Allen).

<u>Navigator</u>—my riding horse is a big, heavy Quarter Horse that reminds me of a knight's charger. He has Three Bars breeding (that's a big deal), but when he picked me, Jonah let him keep me! He's black with rusty rings around his eyes and a rusty muzzle. (Even though he looks black, the proper description is brown, they tell me.) He can find his way home from any place on the island. He's sweet, but no pushover. Just when I think he's sort of a safety net for my beginning riding skills, he tests me.

<u>Joker</u>—Cade's Appaloosa gelding is gray splattered with black spots and has a black mane and tail. He climbs like a mountain goat and always looks like he's having a good time. I think he and Cade have a history, maybe Jonah took them in together?

<u>Biscuit</u>—buckskin gelding, one of Ben's horses, a dependable cow pony. Kit rides him a lot.

<u>Hula Girl</u>—chestnut cutter

<u>Blue Ginger</u>—blue roan mare with tan foal

<u>Honolulu Lulu</u>—bay mare

<u>Tail Afire (Koko)</u>—fudge brown mare with silver mane and tail

<u>Blue Moon</u>—Blue Ginger's baby

<u>Moonfire</u>—Tail Afire's baby

<u>Black Cat</u>—Lady Wong's black foal

<u>Luna Dancer</u>—Hula Girl's bay baby

Honolulu Half Moon

<u>Conch</u>—grulla cow pony, gelding, needs work. Megan rides him sometimes.

<u>Kona</u>—big gray, Jonah's cow horse

<u>Luna</u>—beautiful, full-maned bay stallion is king of 'Iolani Ranch. He and Jonah seem to have a bond.

<u>Lady Wong</u>—dappled gray mare and Kona's dam. Her current foal is Black Cat.

<u>Australian shepherds</u>—pack of five: Bart, Jack, Jill, Peach, and Sass

<u>Pipsqueak/Pip</u>—little shaggy white dog that runs with the big dogs, belongs to Megan and Cathy

<u>Tango</u>—Megan's once-wild rose roan mare. I think she and Hoku are going to be pals.

<u>Sugarfoot</u>—Ann Potter's horse is a beautiful Morab (half Morgan and half Arabian, she told me). He's a caramel-and-white paint with one white foot. He can't be used with "clients" at the Potters' because he's a chaser. Though Ann and her mother, Ramona, have pretty much schooled it out of him, he's still not

quite trustworthy. If he ever chases me, I'm supposed to stand my ground, whoop, and holler. Hope I never have to do it!

<u>Flight</u>—this cremello mare belongs to Aunt Babe (she has a whole herd of cremellos) and nearly died of longing for her missing foal. She was a totally different horse—beautiful and spirited—once she got him back!

<u>Stormbird</u>—Flight's cream-colored (with a blush of palomino) foal with turquoise eyes has had an exciting life for a four-month-old. He's been shipwrecked, washed ashore, fended for himself, and rescued.

<u>Medusa</u>—Black Lava's lead mare—with the heart of a lion—just might be Kit's new horse.

❦ PLACES ❦

<u>Lehua High School</u>—the school Megan and I go to. School colors are red and gold.

<u>Crimson Vale</u>—it's an amazing and magical place, and once I learn my way around, I bet I'll love it. It's like a maze, though. Here's what I know: From town you can go through the valley or take the ridge

road—valley has lily pads, waterfalls, wild horses, and rainbows. The ridge route (Pali?) has sweeping turns that almost made me sick. There are black rock teeter-totter-looking things that are really ancient altars and a SUDDEN drop-off down to a white sand beach. Hawaiian royalty are supposedly buried in the cliffs.

Moku Lio Hihiu—Wild Horse Island, of course!

Mountain to the Sky—sometimes just called Sky Mountain. Goes up to 5,000 feet, sometimes gets snow, and Megan said there used to be wild horses there.

The Two Sisters—cone-shaped "mountains." A borderline between them divides Jonah's land from his sister's—my great-aunt Babe. One of them is an active volcano. Kind of scary.

Sun House—our family place. They call it plantation style, but it's like a sugar plantation, not a Southern mansion. It has an incredible lanai that overlooks pastures all the way to Mountain to the Sky and Two Sisters. Upstairs is this little apartment Jonah built for my mom, but she's never lived in it.

Hapuna—biggest town on island, has airport, flag-pole, public and private schools, etc., palm trees, and coconut trees

<u>'Iolani Ranch</u>—our home ranch. 2,000 acres, the most beautiful place in the world.

<u>Pigtail Fault</u>—Near the active volcano. It looks more like a steam vent to me, but I'm no expert. According to Cade, it got its name because a poor wild pig ended up head down in it and all you could see was his tail. Too sad!

<u>Sugar Sands Cove Resort</u>—Aunt Babe and her polo-player husband, Phillipe, own this resort on the island. It has sparkling white buildings and beaches and a four-star hotel. The most important thing to me is that Sugar Sands Cove Resort has the perfect water-schooling beach for me and Hoku.

❧ ON THE RANCH, THERE ARE ❧
PASTURES WITH NAMES LIKE:

<u>Sugar Mill</u> and <u>Upper Sugar Mill</u>—for cattle

<u>Two Sisters</u>—for young horses, one- and two-year-olds they pretty much leave alone

<u>Flatland</u>—mares and foals

<u>Pearl Pasture</u>—borders the rain forest, mostly two-
and three-year-olds in training

<u>Borderlands</u>—saddle herd and Luna's compound

I guess I should also add me . . .

<u>Darby Leilani Kealoha Carter</u>—I love horses more
than anything, but books come in second. I'm thirteen, and one-quarter Hawaiian, with blue eyes and
black hair down to about the middle of my back. On
a good day, my hair is my best feature. I'm still kind
of skinny, but I don't look as sickly as I did before I
moved here. I think Hawaii's curing my asthma.
Fingers crossed.

I have no idea what I did to land on Wild Horse
Island, but I want to stay here forever.

Darby and Hoku's adventures continue in . . .

MISTWALKER

 Mistwalker

𝓜om loves Hawaii.

She's just forgotten.

The words pounded like a memorized poem. Five syllables matched by five more, they'd drummed a rhythm all day long in Darby Carter's mind.

Excitement over her mother's homecoming had twisted and turned into her sleep, too. In last night's dream, Darby's grandfather Jonah had welcomed her mom home by kissing her cheeks, then slipping a lehua lei over her black hair to settle around her neck.

Mom will forget her feud with Jonah and move back to Wild Horse Island.

If concentrating could make it so, Darby's wish was on its way to coming true.

Ellen Kealoha Carter had sworn never to return to the Hawaiian island where she had grown up, but she was doing it for Darby, to see her honored — along with her friends Megan and Cade — for finding a shipwrecked colt called Stormbird.

The world stood still as Darby watched gold shimmers of sunshine dance over Hoku's vanilla silk mane. Darby didn't even blink until the filly reached her nose under the round pen fence and flapped her lips, reaching for a clump of grass.

Darby caught her breath. She'd tumbled so deep into daydreaming, her mind had wandered away from an important fact: The horse she rode — bareback — was barely trained.

On impulse, her hands tugged at the rope rein leading to Hoku's halter.

Bad move. As Hoku jumped back in surprise, Darby's body wavered like a candle flame someone was trying to blow out.

Slow and gentle. Everything had to be that way with a young horse, especially a young mustang used to running free on the Nevada range.

"It's okay, girl," Darby told Hoku, but her horse pawed the dust with a forefoot.

What would Mom think if she saw us right now? Me and my horse . . .

Darby shook off the question. She'd find out tomorrow, after the presentation at Sugar Sands Cove Resort. Now, at home on 'Iolani Ranch, she'd better focus on riding Hoku.

She let the rein droop, but kept her fingers closed around it. Next, she raised her chin, shrugged her shoulders back, and curved her tailbone toward Hoku's backbone.

The filly shuddered from nose to tail. By the time she realized Hoku was scaring off a fly, not getting ready to buck, Darby's legs had closed on the sorrel's sides.

Naturally, Hoku broke into a trot that made Darby's teeth clack together and her knees clamp tighter.

Hoku rocked into a lope and Darby's mood lifted, even though she'd hoodwinked herself into believing she was a good rider.

If she wanted to keep riding Hoku, it was vital for her mom to decide they should move to Hawaii for good.

She rode with just a halter. For reins, a lead rope was clipped at both ends to the halter ring under Hoku's chin. But tack wasn't important. Darby's body worked with the filly's, sensing the tension and excitement Hoku reflected back to her.

Darby felt the bunched-up muscles in the filly's hindquarters pushing them around the pen. She leaned forward and rested her hands at the base of the filly's neck. Shoulder blades sculpted by generations of range running slid like polished ivory under her fingers as Hoku's legs pulled at the earth.

I love you, she thought as Hoku swept past the corral fence. The ranch yard, Sun House, and green hills slipped by. *And I love this ranch*, she thought as tropical breezes sang through her hair.

Saying that her wild horse was under control made about as much sense as a pirate saying he'd commanded the wind to fill his sails, but Darby didn't care. She was happy.

Hoku settled back to a walk. Her head bobbed from side to side, as if checking each dark-hoofed leg.

Dark hooves were supposed to indicate hard feet, less susceptible to injury.

"You're such a good girl."

The filly's elegant ears pricked forward. At first, Darby thought Hoku was listening to her, but then her horse's head swung toward the crunch of tires.

Who was coming down the ranch road? A rooster tail of dust followed the vehicle and a brown cloud surrounded it. It was probably just the ranch manager, Aunty Cathy, bringing her daughter, Megan, home from school.

Although classes were back in session, school had been chaotic since the mini tsunami. That's what the rest of the world was calling it, but to Darby, there'd been nothing small about it.

Now, workers repaired storm damage and talked of dangerous mold in the school walls that could close the school again. So teachers made the most of each classroom moment, shouting over sawing, hammering, and the blasts of nail guns.

Darby could thank Mr. Potter, her friend Ann's dad, for taking her away from all the racket and driving her home from Lehua High School. It was four o'clock and she'd been riding for half an hour instead of dawdling around school.

Actually, Darby's riding practice was important. Tomorrow her mom would arrive on Wild Horse Island. Ellen had never seen her daughter on a horse.

"We've got to be awesome," Darby told Hoku.

Now Darby recognized the faded red fenders, streaked with rust. It wasn't Aunty Cathy and Megan. It was the farrier's truck.

Hoku's steps slowed. Though the filly was only curious, Darby reined her away from the corral fence.

"No horseshoes for you," Darby assured Hoku.

But then the truck backfired, sounding like a gunshot, and everything happened fast.

Hoku's jump aimed them at the fence rails.

Darby heard the farrier yell, "One-rein stop. Catch her before—"

She knew what he meant, and Darby pulled the left rein toward her knee. She'd done it before, with Navigator, but Hoku didn't react the same way.

Hoku resisted the pull of the rein until her head had to follow. Even then, her body kept moving forward.

Darby slipped left on Hoku's back and caught a sickening glimpse of the cindery dirt below. Scooting forward didn't help her regain her seat. If she held tight with her legs, Hoku would lunge ahead even though her head was aimed in the opposite direction.

Darby had to keep her legs loose or risk bringing them both down.

No way I'll let that happen, Darby promised silently.

She released the left rein. As Hoku straightened and looked ahead once more, Darby braced on her filly's withers, swung her right leg over Hoku's back, then felt frantically for the ground before dropping and landing on both boots.

Eyes wide with confusion, nostrils flared to suck in air, Hoku swung around to face Darby.

"You stopped for me," Darby whispered to her horse. Puzzled and a bit scared, Hoku might have kept running. But Darby had left the filly's back unexpectedly, and it was almost as if she was concerned for her human.

Darby held out a hand, cupped gently, hoping Hoku would come close and rest her chin there.

The white star marking on Hoku's chest rose with the filly's breaths and she looked away.

I'm asking too much, Darby thought.

"Sorry, girl," Darby said. "That was kinda spooky, wasn't it?"

She eased forward to catch the rein. Then she moved alongside her horse and pressed her cheek against Hoku's hot neck.

She wanted to stay like this forever. Breathe in.

Breathe out. Feel the sun kneading the kinks out of their backs, hear trade winds rustling in the trees.

"You be careful there, young lady," the farrier called through the open window of his idling truck. "And get Jonah to show you how to 'whoa' before you 'giddyup.'"

Chuckling, the farrier drove on toward the horses that were tethered outside the tack room.

As if he's not to blame for telling me to make a one-rein stop, Darby glared after him, but it was a good thing she hadn't snapped a comeback, because Hoku was shifting with uneasiness again.

Why had she taken the farrier's shouted advice when she knew her horse better than he—or anyone!—did?

Once more, Darby extended her hand toward her filly's nose, but Hoku's head jerked high and she backed up a few steps, rolling her eyes until they showed white.

Darby relaxed her shoulders, letting her body language tell her horse they were safe, but she wasn't thinking tranquil thoughts.

"What happened to you?" an irritated voice called from behind them.

Darby glanced over her shoulder to see her grandfather standing outside the round pen. Jonah's head, black hair graying at his temples, was cocked to one side.

"Nothing," she said, looking back to Hoku.

"So you're trying to stare that filly into doin' what you say?"

"No, I'm just letting her relax. The truck back-fired, she bolted, and I was losing control. . . ."

Great, Darby thought. She'd better stop talking before she confessed any more.

"So you turned her in circles," Jonah finished her sentence.

He started nodding and Darby guessed he was going to tell her she'd done the right thing.

"No one likes bein' dizzy, 'specially not a horse," Jonah said, then shook his finger at the horse. "That Hoku, she knows she's too big to fall down and get up quick if something's after her."

Darby nodded. "I could feel her trying to keep her balance, but that turning thing? It worked before, when I did it with Navigator."

"He's an experienced horse. He knew goin' around in circles wasn't gettin' him nowhere, so he read your mind and gave you the stop you were after." Jonah shrugged. "You won't see no paniolo trying that merry-go-round stuff."

"What should I have done?" Darby asked.

"Talk to Cade or Kit about bronc stoppin'," Jonah said.

"Bronc stopping? That doesn't sound like some-thing I—"

"Suit yourself," Jonah said. Then his attention shifted to Hoku. "Good the way she stopped for you.

Shows some respect."

Jonah's compliments were so rare, Darby wanted to whoop in celebration, but her grandfather was already walking away.

"I got to go talk to that horseshoein' thief," Jonah muttered, "and tell him to keep his riding advice to himself."

A bronc stop, Darby repeated silently.

Darby led Hoku to the fence.

She had to get back on Hoku and replace the scary backfiring memory with a calm one.

She rode around the corral twice, then managed to open the gate from Hoku's back. She was latching it behind her when light glared in her eyes, making her squint.

Mom? It couldn't be.

Some trick of light made Darby think someone stood on the iron staircase leading up to the apartment over Sun House.

She blinked and no one was there.

Hadn't she just learned a lesson about daydreaming astride a nearly wild horse? But suddenly Darby thought, *How many times has Aunty Cathy offered to let me go through that stuff of Mom's?*

When Ellen Kealoha had left Wild Horse Island, swearing she'd never come back, she'd left some possessions behind. Jonah had stored them in the upstairs apartment he'd built.

Nothing was more important than persuading her

mother to stay on Wild Horse Island. To do that, maybe Darby needed to know why Ellen had left in the first place . . . maybe Darby would find the answers in her mom's old stuff.

She rode Hoku toward the freshly repaired hitching rack, slid off, looped a rope around her filly's neck, and tied her with a secure knot.

Then she started walking quickly toward the apartment stairs, hoping to discover some clues as to why her mom left, and what might convince her to stay.

Discover all the adventures on Wild Horse Island!

HarperTrophy®
An Imprint of HarperCollinsPublishers

www.harpercollinschildrens.com